## Maela awoke, but did not wish to open her eyes.

Her dreams had been so wonderful that even their memory warmed her. Harry had stroked her face and arms as he spoke tender words of love and encouragement. Even now she caught the heady scent of him and inhaled deeply.

"It is well. You can breathe clearly now."

Maela's eyelids felt weighted, but she had to see if it were true. "Harry?" she whispered. His face came into focus. The room seemed filled with light. "Thou art truly here?" Her hand groped in his direction and felt his gentle squeeze.

"You do not remember?"

"I thought 'twas a dream."

"I know not how I will leave thee now that day has dawned, but I care not. Thy fever has broken, and thy cough is productive. I caused you to breathe an herbal mist while you slept. You have coughed up the congestion."

Maela thought this over. It sounded disgusting, but Harry did not look disgusted. "I dreamed. . ." she began. She lifted one arm into view. It was no longer grimy.

Reading her thoughts in her actions, Harry said soberly, "I rubbed thine arms and face with wet cloths, Maela, to bring down the fever. I knew not what else to do."

Maela thought her fever must have returned, for her face burned. Harry rose to prowl about the room. "I feared you would hate me, as you would have no man touch thee."

Far from feeling indignant, Maela wanted to beg for more. "Once you did tend my feet."

"Yea, but this time I did tend thee without thy consent."

"You have ever my full consent, Harry. I trust thee completely. This castle seems a brighter place, for I have seen thy face herein."

**JILL STENGL** makes her home in North Carolina near Seymour Johnson AFB where her husband is stationed. She home schools the three oldest of her four children and also gives piano lessons. Jill began writing when her husband returned from the Gulf War and bought the family's first computer. She writes inspirational romance because that's what she most enjoys reading, and she believes that everything she does should be glorifying to God.

HEARTSONG PRESENTS

**Books by Jill Stengl**
HP197—Eagles Pilot
HP222—Finally, Love

# A Child
# of Promise

*Jill Stengl*

Heartsong Presents

To my home school creative writing class: Erin Arensmeyer, Sarah Finch, Allison Kuhnau, Annie Stengl, Kim Strang, and Rebecca Whitmore. May you always desire to use your talents for God's glory. I love you!

Thank you to Kim Nelson and Paula Pruden-Macha for being blunt and honest, yet kind and encouraging. I couldn't have written this book without you.

**A note from the author:**
*I love to hear from my readers! You may correspond with me by writing:*

**Jill Stengl
Author Relations
PO Box 719
Uhrichsville, OH 44683**

**ISBN 1-57748-405-3**

**A CHILD OF PROMISE**

*Cover illustration by Jocelyn Bouchard.*

PRINTED IN THE U.S.A.

## one

*The young lions do lack, and suffer hunger: but they that
seek the Lord shall not want any good thing.*
Psalm 34:10

A light evening breeze with a lingering hint of winter rustled
the fresh green leaves of ancient beeches, rowans, oaks, and
hazels. Sunlight struggled to pierce hazy gray clouds; the
wildflowers dotting a small clearing lifted their bright heads to
find each infrequent ray. A red squirrel scolded bitterly from
his perch in a crooked oak, disturbed by noisy intruders below.

"Oi! Go to, thou thieving beast!" a laughing voice echoed
through the trees, intermixed with ferocious growls. A small,
scruffy dog gripped one edge of a flat cloth hat between his
sharp teeth while a young man, not long past boyhood, held
the other edge with both hands. Round and round the forest
clearing they spun, the dog growling and tossing his head
from side to side. The hat's owner allowed the dog to tow him
along, his arms swinging loosely though his grip was firm.
"Thought to fool me, did you, Ragwort? Thought to catch me
unaware? Think again, scurvy knave!"

Black, close-cropped hair lifted in the breeze as the man
spun about. Strong white teeth flashed through his sparse
beard. A coarse holland shirt lay open at his brown throat; its
rolled-up sleeves revealed sinewy forearms. Gray woolen
hose hugged long, lean legs; the lacings of his skirted jerkin
hung loose. Rather like a lumbering puppy himself, the young
man sported enormous feet and hands in keeping with a large,
raw-boned frame. He radiated youthful exuberance and good
health.

It was a ludicrous mismatch of strength, yet the tiny dog

appeared to be winning. Another dog, a tall hound, squatted in the grass on the other side of the clearing, its sharp muzzle open in an apparent smile. "Do you also make jest of me, Laitha?" the man called, his tone gentle. The hound dropped to the ground and rolled to her back, wagging her entire rear half.

While watching her antics in pleased surprise, the man slipped on a crushed dockweed. He fell to one knee, then rolled over in the grass, his broad, bony shoulders demolishing more wildflowers. One hand still gripped the hat, and Ragwort redoubled his efforts, fiercely growling as he tugged the man's arm over his head at an awkward angle. The man laughed helplessly, allowing the dog to pull his arm back and forth above his head.

Suddenly the terrier dropped the hat and stared, ears alert. A low "woof" from Laitha brought the man scrambling to his feet. The greyhound stood like a sentinel, her nose pointing in the direction of possible danger—behind the man's back. He spun in place, crouched defensively, one hand reaching to the knife sheath at his side.

At the edge of the clearing stood a pony; on its back perched a girl. A gust of wind rustled the oak towering over her, scattering shadows across the child's white face.

The man relaxed, straightening. "Ah, well met, maiden. What do you seek here?" His voice was pleasant, though he inwardly berated himself for lack of attentiveness.

He presumed that she was of gentle birth, for she possessed a horse and her clothing appeared fine; but closer inspection caused him to wonder. The pony wore neither bridle nor saddle. Bare feet and skinny legs dangled below the ragged edge of the child's kirtle. The grime edging her pale face appeared to be of long standing. Bony wrists extended far beyond the gathered edges of her smock sleeves. Huge dark eyes regarded him with an expression of mingled wonder and apprehension. Was she lost?

"Art thou a wicked man or a good man?"

The low question raised his brows. "A good man, I hope,

though every man has the wicked sin nature within. Why do you ask thusly, child?"

Her eyes narrowed. "Art thou a wizard?"

He sobered. "Nay, I have no such evil craft. I am a bond-servant of Jesus Christ, devoted to His service."

"Thou art a priest, then?"

"Not so, maiden. I am but a simple craftsman. Harry the joiner, at your service." He flourished his rather moist hat and made a graceful bow.

"I saw thee not ere this day. Thou art a foreigner—not of this parish. Do you have leave to encamp upon manor grounds? Sir David Marston does not take kindly to vagabonds." Her tone was formal and proud, and he wondered again about her station.

"I have leave. I am in Sir David's employ, maiden."

"What is thy trade?" Genuine curiosity colored the question, so he excused her impertinence.

"I am a joiner, as I said. I craft woodwork. You are welcome to share my pottage, and I shall play thee a tune upon my lute." Though but a child, she was company.

"I have supped." Belatedly she added, "I thank you," with a respect that had been lacking at first.

Ragwort had by now worked up enough courage to approach her pony and sniff around its hooves. The pony lowered its head and snorted. Ragwort scooted quickly away, barking shrilly. Another low "woof" answered, and the hound moved farther into the clearing, hesitant to approach.

"What ails thy hound?" Bending over her pony's neck, the girl tried to gain a closer view of the dog's face. "It behaves strangely."

"Come near, Laitha." Harry the joiner bent to touch the hound's head as she slowly approached. At first Laitha cringed away, but as he continued to speak softly and stroke her smooth head, she leaned against his leg and heaved a grateful sigh. Her backside began to wiggle as though wagged by a tail, but no tail was visible, only a ragged stump.

Harry looked up to find that the girl had dismounted.

Leading her pony by its forelock, she stepped over a clump of bluebells, her eyes glued to the white hound.

"Speak to Laitha as you approach; she cannot see you," he instructed, still stroking the dog's hard, bony side with one hand.

The child stopped a few feet away, horror twisting her face. "Why, she possesses neither eyes nor ears! What hast thou done to her?"

Laitha cringed, sinking down at Harry's feet. Empty eye sockets gaped with ghastly entreaty as she turned her slender muzzle to her master; pathetic stumps framed naked pink ear canals. "Nay, lass, the child shall harm thee not," Harry crooned, his hands caressing the dog's head, which had once been attractive, marked with brindled patches over each eye and ear.

"Last Michaelmas I came upon Laitha in Epping Forest, blood soaked and nigh death. I can only guess wherefore. Perhaps she angered a lord with timidity on the stag hunt; perhaps she made chase to a hare; perhaps she was simply too slow."

Dropping the pony's forelock, the girl sat down tailor fashion and reached out to the dog. "Laitha," she called, her low voice pleading. "Come hither, Laitha. I will harm thee not." Patiently she coaxed while Harry studied her.

Her laced waistcoat and kirtle of cranberry red were torn and faded, the embroidered edging missing many threads. Her soiled cap slipped back to reveal greasy hair of an indeterminate hue. Was it red? Odd, with those dark eyes. Long, slender fingers wiggled as she entreated the dog to come to her. These were not the hands of a peasant child.

The little terrier made the first move. Quivering tail held like a pikestaff over his back, he took cautious steps closer to those outstretched fingers, his black nose twitching. Soon he was happily seated in her lap, his pink tongue lolling as she scratched his wiry back. Laitha still pressed against the joiner's leg.

"You have charmed Ragwort," Harry observed. "He has

eyes to behold thine honest face."

"Alas for Laitha!" she sighed. "Do you think she will e'er trust another?"

"I know not. Perchance in time you shall win her."

Ragwort's button eyes twinkled merrily. The girl's lips softened in the first semblance of a smile. "Ragwort pleases me."

"And you please him." Harry smiled. "Tell me thy name," he ordered gently.

Those dark eyes flew to his face, alert and suspicious once again; but after a careful search of his countenance the child replied, "I am called Maela."

"May Ella?"

"Nay, Maela." Her eyes narrowed. "Ishmaela Andromeda Trenton."

Under that challenging glare he dared not smile. " 'Tis a pleasure to make thine acquaintance, my lady." This designation must certainly accompany her surname. Trenton was the nearest village, and ancient Castle Trent dominated the local skyline.

But her lips curled. "I am no lady." Gently dumping Ragwort from her lap, she leaped to her feet and marched across the clearing, leaving her pony to graze at will. Harry looked from her to the pony, then, tugging its forelock, led the obliging little horse after its mistress.

Maela headed directly for Harry's small camp and stood with hands on hips to survey it. An empty two-wheeled cart leaned on its shafts beside a crate of clucking chickens. A woolly spotted donkey lifted its head, letting out a raspy bray in greeting. Beside the makings of a fire rested an assortment of iron pots and utensils, a few wooden bowls and spoons, and a smooth board. A bucket full of vegetables waited where Harry had left it to chase Ragwort.

"You dwell here among the trees? Why not at the manor with other hirelings?"

"I prefer peace and solitude to noise and squalor," he explained. "I sleep alone and care for mine own needs."

Releasing the pony, he began chopping vegetables for his pottage, squatting beside the iron pot of water. The dogs flopped down beneath the cart, Laitha's head resting across Ragwort's back.

"You cook? Mend thine own clothes?"

"What I do not for myself, I purchase or take in trade."

The child shook her head. "What manner of man is this? Never heard I of one such." She sounded disapproving, yet admiring. "You have need of nothing and no one."

"Nay, not so."

"What do you mean?"

"I have need of the Lord God. It is He that provides mine every need, as He promised in His Word. Lions do lack and suffer hunger, but they that seek the Lord shall not want any good thing."

She did not respond. Those eyes watched his every move.

"What age have you, child?"

"Thirteen last January. And you?"

"Nineteen last March. I had guessed thee at ten years."

"And I took thee for a man grown!"

He frowned, though his lips twisted in amusement. "I am a man grown. I have been on mine own these many years."

"You do rove about the land as a vagrant?"

His reply dripped with irony. "I do pause to lay hand upon work now and again. I made acquaintance with Sir David last summer while at DeHaven Park, Lord Weston's estate in Essex. I did, at that time, carve rampant lions atop the newel posts of the great staircase. Sir David Marston repeatedly expressed his desire of a carved screen for his minstrel gallery and frequently lamented the dearth of skilled joiners in his county—hence my presence in Suffolk. I move farther north, closer to home, with each position I accept, it seems. Soon I hope to visit my family. I have not seen them in many a year."

"Where is thy home?"

"Near Lincoln."

"I would hear of thy travels. Have you been to London?" She sat upon a handy log, obviously intending to stay awhile.

"Yea, I have even seen our queen at a short distance. Once she did stop and take the hand of a man near me and smile and talk to him. She is delicate and pale, like thee, and yet," Harry frowned thoughtfully as he studied Maela's face again, "yet your features, though similar in color, are unlike."

Maela sighed. "And she is reputed a beauty. Tush!" she brushed it aside. " 'Tis of little moment. Do you admire life at court?"

Harry chuckled. "Court life I know nothing of, for I move not in that sphere. I am a hired artisan, not among the gentry, Maela. And I care not for town life. The smells—phew!" He shook his head in disgust. "And the plague! I took me off afore the worst of the plague hit, yet many a red cross I saw upon doors in the leaving."

Maela leaned forward, bony elbows upon her knees. "Have you beheld the Black One?"

"Eh? Which black what?" He picked up an onion and peeled off the papery skin.

"Grandmere says that when plague takes a man, the Black One takes his soul out the front door! She did witness it." The girl's slight frame shivered. "I dread this frightful sight!"

"Maela, the plague is but a sickness, not a curse. I believe 'tis caused by filth. If people bathed often and laundered their clothing, mayhap these illnesses would strike not."

The child gaped. "Surely thou art mad! Bathe often? Bathing chills the lungs and brings on fever! I bathe only twice a year, as Grandmere bids me."

"I see," he murmured, and might have added, "so I smell," for an occasional ill wind had already told him that the child reeked. Her sentiments about bathing were not uncommon; Harry had met few people in England who shared his unorthodox views about hygiene.

"I bathe frequently," he informed her, "and I perish not of lung fever. In truth, I am seldom ill."

She was silent for several moments, watching his nimble fingers slice the last few parsnips and drop them into the pot. "Thou art a strange man."

Harry lit a pile of tinder with a few expert strokes of his flint. Blowing and carefully feeding the flame with dry twigs, he soon had a large enough fire to cook his pottage. Hanging the pot upon a sturdy framework, he suspended it over the fire. Still sprinkling herbs into the pottage, he casually asked, "Will you take a cup of milk?"

"Whence comes this milk?"

"A gift of love from Genevieve," he grinned.

"Genevieve?" Lines appeared between her dark brows. "I thought you slept alone."

"So I do. Genevieve sleeps with Samson, though they are merely friends." He uttered a short yodeling call, and an answering bleat came from behind the cart. With a scramble of legs, a small brown goat rose to its feet and bleated again.

"Genevieve—a gift from a grateful employer. Her milk is a wondrous addition to my meals. No longer must I drink only ale and beer. A kid shall birth come summer." He watched the child make acquaintance with his goat. It was abundantly clear that beasts were Maela's passion in life.

"Samson is the ass's name. What do you call the fowl?" She leaned over the crate to inspect his chickens.

"Sage, Parsley, and Rosemary. It keeps them humble."

A gurgle of laughter rewarded him. "You would not eat them?" she sounded slightly concerned.

"Nay. They provide eggs."

Harry rose to release his three hens and encouraged the girl to scatter their grain. She squatted down to stroke their soft feathers, pleased when the friendly birds allowed her caresses. "These also were gifts?"

"Accepted in payment for services rendered, more like."

"Do you not fear to lose them? Stoats, foxes, and thieves abound hereabouts, and you have little protection."

"The Lord watches over me," he assured her. "I own little of value, but I will fight for my possessions."

"Art thou armed?" she asked, eyes widening.

"I am armed sufficiently." He smiled. "Few venture to accost me."

Her eyes flitted over his rangy frame from head to toe. "One would not. Two might try, and from cover."

"Leave them try. No arrow may take my life unless the Lord allows." Returning to the fire, he stirred the pottage, sniffing the steam.

Maela's small nose twitched like Ragwort's. "Truly, you do cook well," she wavered. "Grandmere's pottage lacks flavor. Have you enough for me?"

He looked down at the full pot, then lifted one eyebrow in her direction. " 'Twill suffice."

Maela consumed an astounding amount of pottage, and Harry polished off several full bowls, yet the pot was still partially full when they had finished eating. Harry offered more bread, but Maela clutched her stomach, shaking her head. "Nay, I would surely burst. I have not eaten so well since. . ." She paused, then shook her head. "I cannot think when."

He indicated the waiting dogs. "Rag and Laitha would eat our leavings. You may give them sup."

The words were scarcely out of his mouth before she had refilled her bowl and placed it before the dogs. They ate together, one at each side of the bowl, while Maela crouched beside them, fascinated. Once the bowl was empty, Ragwort licked Laitha's muzzle with almost motherly tenderness. Unable to express her feelings with tail or ears, the hound whined softly, enjoying her friend's attentions.

"They have a great love," Maela observed wistfully. Firelight flickered across her face, for the forest grew dark.

Harry smiled at her, his eyes kind. He was startled at the brilliance of the smile she returned, having grown accustomed to her sober expression.

"You will abide here, Harry Joiner?" she asked. "I may visit thee again?"

The passion in her request took him aback. "Surely you may return, child. I shall wrap these soft rolls and a pasty for thee to take and enjoy at thy leisure. Dovie, the cook at Marston Hall, baked them," he remarked to lighten the conversation. "Do you know her? A comely maid and excellent cook."

Maela's face darkened abruptly. "I know her not."

Harry went on, thoughtfully stirring the fire, "I considered not my words. A lady of Castle Trent would not know a cook. You dwell at the castle?"

Maela nodded shortly, her expression guarded.

"Art thou related to Sir Hanover Trenton? His son visited Fulbrook Manor in Hertfordshire where I carved the drawing room paneling two seasons past. A goodly lad he is, though harsh with his pony. Isaac Trenton. . ." he paused, finally noticing the girl's stiffened shoulders. "Thy brother? Cousin?"

Maela abruptly sprang to her feet and flung herself at the grazing pony. Apparently used to his mistress's unpredictable whims, the pony hardly batted an eye, allowing her to scramble upon his broad back. She dug bare heels into his sides and wheeled him away.

"Maela, tarry! I would escort thee home—" Harry leaped to intercept her, but he was too late. Thudding hoofbeats faded into the darkness. His arms fell to his sides; his mouth slowly closed. Attempting to track her in this strange forest would be useless. "Lord Jesus, bring the child safely home, I pray Thee," he spoke softly, his face upturned into a falling mist.

He returned to the fireside, his eyes troubled. "What did I say to offend her?" Ragwort looked as puzzled as Harry felt; Laitha looked blank, her mutilated face revealing no thoughts.

Harry caught his sleepy hens, moved Samson's stake closer to the cart beside the goat, and banked the fire. "Tomorrow I shall inquire about the waif," he muttered, yet misgivings assailed him. With increased knowledge might also come an increased sense of responsibility. "Lord, what wouldst Thou have me to do?"

He retired early, rolling into his blankets beneath the partial shelter of the cart. The dogs crowded under the blankets on either side of him. Misty rain fell all that night, but he paid it no heed.

# two

*If any of you lack wisdom, let him ask of God,*
*that giveth to all men liberally. . .and it shall be given him.*
James 1:5

Harry woke early the next morning, to his mild annoyance. His face was cold, but warmth radiated from the dogs at his sides. Laitha snored softly and whimpered in her sleep, the probable cause of his early awakening. He wrapped an arm around the dog. Laitha suffered from the cold, her short coat affording little protection. She deserved to spend her remaining days by a warm hearth, dreaming of past hunts. A blinded sight-hound—could anything be more pathetic? Never again would the great dog stretch her long legs to race through fen and forest. Mankind's cruelty to dumb beasts at times caused Harry shame—yet even more appalling was man's inhumanity to man.

Maela sprang to his mind. Though she was well-spoken and mannerly, the child's furtive expression, ragged clothing, and bruised face bespoke neglect and harsh treatment. His eyes drifted to the log, dimly visible in the morning half-light, where she had perched the night before. Her slight figure and ethereal smile now seemed a figment of his lonely imagination. Yet, would he have imagined the dirt and the smell?

"Lord, didst Thou bring me to dwell in this place for a deeper purpose than the carving of a gallery screen? I have questioned my wisdom in accepting the position—for this lack of proper accommodations is an onerous trial—yet I did believe, and believe still, that Thou didst desire me to take it." Harry often prayed aloud while alone. "Guide me, Lord, for I am at a loss."

After a breakfast of boiled eggs, porridge, raisins, wild strawberries, and a large mug of Genevieve's milk, Harry extracted his greatest treasure, a Coverdale Bible, from his small clothes chest. In the book of Ephesians he located the Apostle Paul's concise description of a believer's behavior. It was difficult to read in the gray twilight beneath the trees, but Harry's memory filled in the blanks.

As he read, he prayed, requesting strength for the day to live as God pleased. "Let me not grieve Thy Spirit with corrupt speech or wicked thoughts. Help me to forgive others as Thou hast forgiven me and to walk in love. Purify my heart from filthiness and foolish, coarse talk, and fill me with Thy goodness. I go before my fellow workers, the maidens, the gentry, and every human creature I meet today as Thine emissary."

An unpleasant thought struck him. "Surely Thou wouldst not have me to dwell among the servants, Lord. The manor garrets are crowded and noisome. I can function as emissary from here."

He argued aloud with the persistent, silent Voice. "Nay, I do not consider myself above them, but. . .Yea, I know Thou hast commissioned me as salt and light to the world, and yet. . ."

His shoulders slumped. "Verily, I can deny Thee nothing; for Thy sake I can endure even this. I shall move my possessions to the hall this very day."

This was a momentous surrender indeed, for Harry cherished his privacy.

Harry packed up his camp and cared for his beasts. After hitching Samson, he loaded the chicken crate and his few possessions into the cart.

"Come," he ordered the dogs, and set off without a backward glance, walking at Samson's side. The beast seldom needed prodding; he enjoyed Harry's company. Genevieve, tethered behind the cart, trotted in its wake.

Marston Hall loomed out of the morning mist. Harry approached it from the rear, but the great manor house was impressive from any angle. Half-timbered with many glass windows, the magnificent hall blended aesthetically into the surrounding green fields and lush forest.

Dogs rushed to greet the small cavalcade as Harry picketed his beasts beside the carp pond. Laitha and Ragwort bristled, stiff-legged and alert. Upon recognizing Harry, the manor mastiffs and hounds relaxed. Soon all tails wagged, noses sniffed, and invitations to play were issued. Harry smiled as he watched. It was good to see Laitha accepted as an equal, though she could not join their romps. Ragwort was dwarfed by his new playmates, but he didn't seem to notice. Harry hoped none of them would crush the terrier by mistake.

"Good morrow, Joiner."

Harry turned to see Marston's headman approaching. "God give you good day, Goodman Lyttleton."

"I bring news," Lyttleton went on without pause. "The master has requested thee to abide in the woodman's cottage near the oak coppice rather than hide out in the forest like a bandit. It needs repair, but he will provide lumber and thatch, if you will do the work. There is grazing for thy stock, and room for a kitchen garden behind."

For a moment, Harry could only stand amazed at God's incredible sense of timing and humor. He recalled seeing the cottage, a ramshackle one-room dwelling, located not far from his favorite camp. "I accept this generous offer with many thanks."

Amused smiles flickered across Harry's lips as he worked that day. He should not have been surprised, really, for Sir David Marston was a kindly, generous country squire, and God was certainly never behindhand with His blessings. Had he only surrendered his will sooner, he might have been ensconced in the cottage by this time! Harry was eager to explore his new home. He felt ashamed, now, of his stubborn refusal to mingle with the manor servants, but God had made the best of the situation; and, Harry realized, had he dwelt at the manor, he would not have encountered Maela.

Maela. He had almost forgotten to ask about her.

"Have you met such a person?" was Dovie's answer when

he questioned her at dinner. She did not appreciate his topic of conversation. For days Harry had taken the noon meal in the cook's company, and he seemed to admire her; but always he seemed out of her reach in a way Dovie could not understand.

"Yea, of a truth, in the wood yesterday. She has the appearance and manner of gentry, yet her clothing is in rags. Has Sir Hanover Trenton a daughter?"

Dovie gave an affected giggle and spoke rapidly with great animation. Her hands fluttered about, frequently caressing Harry's arm or chest. "Speakest thou in earnest or in jest? Sir Hanover has a son, not a daughter. Do you know that he is a courtier of the queen? He is an important man. The castle is but one of his many estates. He seldom journeys hence, for of late the castle has little to offer—yet I tell you plain, he comes within a fortnight. When in the vicinity, Sir Hanover lodges with Bishop Carmichael at Parminster Court."

"Indeed," Harry remarked. "He ne'er abides in the castle?"

"I think not." Dovie batted her big eyes and retied the drawstring of Harry's shirt. To her irritation, he wasn't even looking her way. He munched on a handful of almonds and relaxed against the bench back. They were alone in a kitchen corner, hidden from the chattering maids and field hands by a row of tall milk cans.

"Is Castle Trent deserted?"

"Nay, it has a few retainers. Dobbin Titwhistle collects rent from tenants, and Hera Coats, the witch, watches over the keep. A few old servants remain in the outbuildings for lack of better position."

"Did you say 'witch'?"

"Yea, in truth. Every man fears to cross her path, though sundry seek her out for spells and potions. She ne'er attends church, yet no churchwarden dares demand a fine lest she place a curse upon him! She once gave our vicar the evil eye and caused his horse to go lame."

Harry believed her. The vicar had not so far impressed him with either intelligence or sincerity. He seemed the type to lend credulity to the curses of a village witch.

"I would have Mistress Coats prescribe thee a love potion, for thy heart gives me little notice!" Dovie leaned close, her eyes serious. "Leave off this incessant talk of castle affairs! Give me thy full regard, for I would know thee well, Harry Jameson."

Now she had Harry's undivided attention.

"I hear you have been provided a cottage, Harry. Couldst thou use mine aid setting it to rights?" She playfully walked two fingers up his chest and cupped his bearded cheek in her hand. "I would accompany thee hence at eventide." Heavy lashes fluttered as she lifted inviting eyes.

"Nay, I need no such aid!" Harry leaped up, nearly fell over the milk cans, and fairly ran from the kitchen.

Safely back in the woodshed, he berated himself for a fool. Dovie was obviously practiced at using those big cow eyes and her shapely body to entice men. He had been foolish to spend time in her company.

"Thou hast removed scales from mine eyes, Lord! It is well, in truth, that I shall not live at the manor. Dovie is unlikely to frequent the coppice cottage, for it is a fair distance. Indeed, Thou doest all things well."

Tense and somewhat rattled, he felt in need of vigorous work. Simon, the ancient woodsman, as gnarled as the oak trees he husbanded with tender care, discovered Harry behind the woodshed, pounding on a knot-ridden hickory log.

"Harry, thou couldst better use thy skills. His lordship pays thee to carve wood, not hack it to kindling," the old man chuckled.

Harry's mallet dropped to his side, and he jerked the adze from the half-split log. "True enough, Simon." He wiped one arm across his forehead. He had stripped off his jerkin to work in his shirtsleeves. It was not a hot day, but Harry was overheated. His chest heaved in a sigh; sweat trickled down his temples.

"Have you a burden upon your heart?"

Loath to speak of his misadventures with Dovie, Harry instead broached the subject of Maela. "I met a child, a gently

born child in tattered raiment. She claims the name Trenton. I
would learn more of her."

"A maid child, you say?" Simon mused. "Artemis Coats's
daughter, no doubt."

"Coats! Is the child mad, then, to claim kinship with
Trenton?"

Simon rubbed his rough hands together. "Did she appear
mad?"

"Nay, she appeared intelligent and sane," Harry admitted.

"Her claim is valid, though not legal. I know the Coats
family of old."

Harry nodded. "Continue."

"Sir Hanover Trenton has a wife who resides at another of
his properties, near London. Notwithstanding, while lodging
at Castle Trent, his lordship went in unto the damsel Artemis,
daughter of a servant. In time she was found with child, and
Sir Hanover was filled with joy, for his wife was barren. His
lordship intended to make the child his heir, but alas! His
wife also conceived a child. Artemis delivered a girl child,
but the wife presented Sir Hanover with a son."

"Isaac Trenton," Harry murmured, suddenly understanding
Ishmaela's reaction and the significance of her name.
"Artemis named her daughter Ishmaela, knowing that Isaac
was the child of promise."

"If you claim acquaintance with the child, she must yet
live, though her mother died years since."

Harry's eyes were vacant. He was recalling Ishmaela's
betraying statement, "I am no lady," and her evident hunger
for love and friendship. "Poor little waif," he sighed.

"Attend upon me now, leave the wench alone, Harry. If Sir
Hanover wishes me to think her dead, then dead she is. I
would not cross the desires of the gentry."

But Harry's thoughts were far away. The afternoon was
waning; soon he would be on his way to the cottage. Would
Ishmaela return to the clearing? He would have to look for
her, just in case.

# three

*Therefore if any man be in Christ, he is a new creature:*
*old things are passed away; behold,*
*all things are become new.*
2 Cor. 5:17

Marston made good his promise; stacks of lumber and thatching reeds awaited Harry when he arrived at the cottage that evening. It was, actually, little more than a pink wattle and daub shack with a small livestock shed and fenced clearing at the rear. Its rotted thatching had caved in at one place near the peak of the steep roof. No chimney emerged through the blackened thatch, for the cottage had no proper fireplace, only a charred depression in the center of its dirt floor.

Harry took a quick glance around the filthy interior. "It has. . . potential."

He left his possessions and livestock in the weed-choked yard and set out for the clearing with the dogs at his side. Ragwort barked for joy, and even Laitha let out a yelp or two. All day long they had watched over Harry's possessions, waiting beside the fishpond for their master to finish his work.

"No longer, my friends," Harry told them. "We now possess a cottage and garden. No more traveling to and fro; no more vagrancy."

If only that were true. For many months now, Harry had wanted to settle, to possess a free-holding of his own. He wanted a wife, children, and a community wherein he would not be always considered a foreigner, an interloper. He greatly missed his family—especially his mother.

At the tender age of thirteen, he had left school to be

apprenticed to an itinerant master joiner. Three years later, in Lancashire, Master Wilson Tupper had suddenly died, leaving his apprentice to complete their current project alone. Harry not only completed the mahogany mantelpiece; he improved upon his master's work. Impressed and amazed by the boy's genius, his employer had recommended him to several friends. Never since had Harry lacked for work—indeed, he could not meet the demand for his exquisite carvings.

But a traveling artisan's life did not offer the stability Harry craved.

Ishmaela's pony grazed contentedly beneath a spreading tree. Lifting its head at Harry's approach, it whinnied, sniffing noses with Ragwort, who still kept a wary eye on its hooves.

"How now?" Harry greeted the friendly creature, patting its shedding neck. A cloud of chestnut hair rose beneath his hand.

"His name is Pegasus," advised a voice from above. Harry looked up into the branches of the oak, but saw nothing at first. A pixie face peeked from around a huge bough, and Maela giggled. "Fooled you, did I not?"

Warmth welled up in Harry's big heart. "Yea, of a truth, you fooled me, child."

Kirtle hitched into her sash, Maela showed most of her skinny white legs as she nimbly scrambled down the tree. Harry averted his eyes, dismayed by her lack of modesty.

Retying her cap strings, Maela skipped up to him, then fell to her knees to greet the dogs. Ragwort covered her face with moist kisses. Laitha still hesitated to approach, though she showed some desire to meet the child who called her name in such caressing tones.

Maela looked up into Harry's eyes and smiled.

"Come hither." Harry held out a hand, but Maela only looked at it, then at his face.

"Do you not wish to see my new dwelling? Sir David presented me with a cottage this day, and it needs work aplenty ere I sleep in it."

Maela rose in a fluid motion, but made no move to accept

his hand. She called her pony, which came to her with bobbing head and a soft snort. Taking him by the forelock, she looked up at Harry.

Harry turned to lead the way to his new home, telling her the story of its acquisition as he walked. Maela strolled along beside him. She said nothing, but once when Harry looked at her she smiled again. He noticed that her teeth were straight and even, though as dirty as the rest of her. Why they had not rotted was the question.

Stopping before the ramshackle cottage, Harry gave a sweep of one arm. "Thou art welcome to my humble dwelling, but I commend thee not to enter ere the roof be mended. The present thatch is occupied, I fear."

"You will need a canopy upon thy bed." Maela giggled as she pushed over the gate to the livestock pen and herded her pony inside. Genevieve had made good headway against the weeds in Harry's absence.

He smiled. "No doubt, lest my slumber be disturbed by enterprising mice." Watching her fondle Samson and Genevieve, he wondered what subject to discuss next. He could not bring up the subject of her parentage unless he wished a repeat performance of last night's hasty exit.

Turning from the animals with a happy sigh, she inquired, "What wouldst thou have me to do? I would help thee."

He floundered for a moment. "Uh, you may sweep rubbish from the yard while I replace this gate."

"Have you a broom?" Maela approached the cart. At his affirmative reply, she dug through his tools until she found the old twig broom, then proceeded to sweep the yard. Following her industrious lead, Harry set to work, building a new gate for the livestock pen.

Conversation would have been difficult, so Harry began to sing as he worked, filling Maela's wondering ears with ballads and hymns. His medium tenor voice was sweet and clear.

Her work completed, Maela busied herself with freeing the chickens, scattering their grain, and brushing the donkey and the pony. "May I milk Genevieve?"

He stopped filing for a moment. "Have you milked a goat before?"

"Never."

"I will teach you." Laying aside the nearly finished gate, he rose, brushing shavings from his hose. Lifting his elbows and flexing his shoulders, he stretched, groaning softly. "A long day," he explained to his waiting audience of one.

She nodded, looking sympathetic.

"I'll begin supper soon. Tonight we have a coney for our pottage. There was game to spare at the manor this day." He rubbed his belly, and Maela smiled, rubbing her middle in imitation.

Genevieve was more than willing to be milked. Harry tied her to one of the few solid posts in sight, then settled on a stool at her side. Placing a wooden bowl beneath her swollen udder, he showed Maela how to pinch off the teat, then push out the milk with her remaining fingers. Milk foamed into the bowl.

Maela clasped her hands at her breast in delight. "May I try?"

Harry vacated the stool, but stayed close. Maela patted the curious goat, then reached for the firm udder. Taking one teat in hand, she tried to squeeze it off, but her small fingers could not reach, and only a trickle of milk rewarded her effort.

Genevieve stamped impatiently, narrowly missing the bowl.

"Here." Harry squatted and placed his hand on top of Maela's to pinch off the teat for her. "Now squeeze gently." He felt the warmth of her little body beside him. The foul odor was intense, but he bravely ignored it.

She didn't move. Glancing down at her, he was startled to see her eyes squeezed shut. Every muscle and nerve in her body was strung taut. "Maela? What ails thee?"

With a suddenness that knocked him off his feet, she flung her arms around his neck and squeezed. For an instant he thought she had attacked him, but when his hand touched her quaking shoulder he realized that this was a hug, a sign of trust and affection.

Sitting in the dirt, he patted a protruding shoulder blade, not knowing what to say. She knelt before him, her arms squeezing tight, her dirty cap resting on his shoulder. Gently he reminded, "Genevieve awaits thee, child."

Maela nodded, wiped her nose and eyes on one sleeve, and turned back to the goat. This time, with Harry's help, she managed to squeeze several good streams of milk from Genevieve's udder. With a satisfied smile, she surrendered her stool and watched Harry finish the job.

"May I milk her again next day?"

"Perhaps. 'Tis time to prepare our coney stew, lest we starve."

While Harry built the fire in a cleared space in the yard, then gutted and skinned out the rabbit, Maela made herself useful by washing and chopping the vegetables. Harry stole frequent glances at her intent expression as she worked. In spite of the dirt and the smell, she was an appealing creature. Those big dark eyes and black brows were startling against her white skin, and her turned-up nose gave her a saucy look. Never before had he seen such an adorable mouth. Her lips were smooth and full, and a deep dent above her upper lip gave the impression that she was perpetually puckering up for a kiss. She seemed younger than thirteen, perhaps due to her diminutive size.

"Tell me about thy family," Maela ordered, scooping chopped leeks into the pot.

"My father is the youngest son of a Spanish nobleman."

Maela's jaw dropped. "Indeed?"

"He was destined for the Roman church but could not accept its teachings, so he fled to England. King Henry was yet living at the time, and a Protestant Spaniard was acceptable company, even in Lincolnshire. He wed Susan Dixon, a yeoman's daughter, purchased property in the Wolds, and became a sheep husbandman. He is a fine, godly man, upright in all his ways."

"And thy mother?"

Harry's expression softened. "My mother is fair beyond

description. She did weep copiously at my departure, and that is nigh six years since. Mine eyes ache to behold her lovely face once more."

"Why have you not hitherto returned?"

Harry chopped the rabbit into large chunks and dropped it into the simmering pot. "They cannot support me, and I cannot earn my keep as joiner there, for manor houses and fine churches are scarce." He rose to his full height, eyes fixed upon the distance, and revealed a dream, "I would settle in Lincolnshire someday on a free-holding of mine own. I had planned to depart hence this season, but I accepted Marston's offer. . ."

"Had you traveled home, I would know thee not," Maela mused softly.

Harry met her gaze across the fire. "God planned us to meet," he stated firmly. "He loves thee, Maela, and He desires that thou shouldst know Him."

Maela stared at him, her expression quizzical but open. "Wherefore say you that He loves me? I know Him not. Grandmere says He is cruel and harsh and sends men to hell."

"Do you trust and love thy grandmother?" Harry asked, wondering about her relationship with the "witch."

The child's shoulders hunched, and she cast frightened looks around. "I love her not. Should she discover that I am here, she would send plague upon thee."

"Thy grandmother has no power over me. My God is greater far than any power here on earth. He would be thy God as well, and protect thee. After we sup, would you hear more of Him?"

Maela nodded, one hand pressed to her flat breast.

Harry read to Maela by firelight that evening, seated upon logs beside the fire. Page after page he turned, until at last Matthew's gospel had ended.

Maela waited, hoping for more. "Is that all?"

"Nay, but 'tis sufficient for the night. Shall you be missed at the castle?"

Maela shook her head.

"May I accompany thee home?"

Her hand fluttered to her breast again, a movement he now recognized as an attempt to calm a fast-beating heart. "Part way," she allowed, unable to entirely reject his offer.

Harry walked beside her pony along the dark road. Perhaps the darkness made her feel safe, or perhaps the late hour loosened her tongue, for Maela became unaccountably talkative as they walked. "When I was a child my grandmere did watch me like a cat watches a mouse and screech at me for every fault, but since Mother's death, Grandmere frequents the wine cellar. She knows not of mine absence."

"And Master Titwhistle?" A name like that was not quickly forgotten.

"I allow not Dob to see me—ever. He twists mine arms and hurts me. I did not think a man could be kind until I saw thee at play with Ragwort."

Maela shifted on her pony, swinging her legs forward over Pegasus's shoulders. "Men that laugh are wicked men—yet Harry is not wicked, and he laughs often. Good men smile not and hate childer—yet Harry is good, and he smiles oft and is kind to childer. I think, Maela," she addressed herself, "that Harry's God is not the god of Bishop Carmichael. Harry's Jesus makes him beautiful."

Harry spoke softly, half afraid to interrupt her soliloquy. "Heed thyself, Maela. Harry's Jesus can be Maela's Jesus, and make her into a new creature also."

Maela was quiet for a moment. "I would hear more of Jesus on the morrow. Did you write the stories, Harry?"

Though amazed by her ignorance, Harry answered calmly, "Nay. Long ago, men who knew Jesus when He was on earth wrote the stories. They are true stories, Maela. The men who wrote them died for the truth when men that hated Jesus tried to make them recant."

Maela nodded. "They would die not for the stories had they invented them."

Her simple wisdom surprised Harry. "That is doubtless true."

"They were men such as thee, Harry. I love them, and I love Jesus. Would that I might embrace Him as I embraced thee!"

Harry's heart melted into a puddle. "Maela, thou art the sweetest child."

"Lovest thou me, Harry?"

Taken aback, Harry stammered, "Why. . .to be sure. . .I am ever thy friend, Maela."

"None has loved me since my mother died, Harry. I knew not that a man could love."

Harry knew he was treading on eggshells. "Thy father?"

"He has a son to love and cares nothing for a girl child. When he comes from London, he brings me fancy clothes to wear while I play the recorder and dance for his companions. He will come again soon. Would that I could hide until they are gone away!"

"They do not. . .harm thee?" Harry asked hesitantly.

Her voice was haughty at first, then died to a near whisper, "I let no man touch me. Nevertheless they speak words I do not understand and laugh together. There is much evil in the castle when they are about."

Pegasus halted abruptly. Harry wondered how Maela signaled her pony without a bridle. "You must stop here. Dob would kill thee should he discover thee on castle grounds."

"Thou art safe, Maela?"

"Yea." Without another word, she cued her pony and cantered down a side road, vanishing into the shadows.

## four

*The angel of the Lord encampeth round about them
that fear him, and delivereth them.*
Psalm 34:7

While Harry shopped one morning several weeks later, a group of noblemen rode past the marketplace. Supremely ignoring the common folk surrounding them, they talked and laughed loudly. Their horses' hooves clopped on the rude cobblestones. Servants, more modestly clothed and mounted, followed behind. A pack of hounds trotted among the horses, wagging, yelling, casting about, soiling the already filthy streets.

Harry watched them pass. One of these men might be Maela's father. Harry shook his head slightly, finding it difficult to comprehend the connection between ragged little Maela and these gentry in their rich garb. Where would they be going this morning? On a hunt, most likely. The jolly group turned down a side street and passed out of his view.

Maela had not returned to Harry's cottage. He had hoped to see her at church, but she did not appear. No chestnut pony grazed in the meadow; no sprightly monkey climbed the ancient trees. While in town, Harry searched the streets for any sign of the girl, with no success. He could not seem to help worrying about her. Was her father treating her well?

In saner moments he admitted that quite possibly he would never see her again, and, at any rate, her fate was out of his control. God would have to handle this one without Harry's help. Maela's situation was difficult, but far from rare. Many noblemen sired illegitimate children, and many of these children fared well for themselves. Perhaps Sir Hanover would arrange an advantageous marriage for his pretty daughter.

Such things had been known to happen—but this knowledge gave Harry no comfort.

Around Harry, market vendors touted their wares in stentorian chant. People pushed, shoved, and cursed, vying for the finest wares, dickering for the lowest prices. Children on their mothers' hips wailed; donkeys loaded with bundles brayed. Chickens cackled and pigeons cooed from their cages. The stench of blood and flesh was nearly overpowered by the reek of rotting fruit, animal waste, and unwashed bodies. Market day—an adventure for the senses.

Feeling eyes upon his back, Harry turned abruptly, but saw nothing untoward. A man staggered past him and belched loudly. Two large dogs circled beneath the fishmonger's table, hackles raised, teeth bared. Harry was glad he had left his dogs at the cottage. A house sparrow hopped boldly along the cobblestones, searching for crumbs.

Frowning, Harry resumed his business of selecting a fresh roast, brushing flies from a promising cut. "Art thou certain the lamb was slaughtered this day?" he asked skeptically.

"Ye say full true," the butcher responded, looking affronted at the question. "This very morn at dawn."

Catching a furtive movement from the corner of his eye, Harry glanced toward the next stall and caught sight of a dirty little hand sliding a peach from a stack on the table. Hand and peach quickly disappeared from view.

"Wrap it. I shall return," Harry assured the butcher, then ducked around the booth in time to spot a flash of red petticoat whisking between the flowerseller's and the cobbler's booths. Harry could not squeeze between people and carts as easily as a child could, but his long legs overtook the girl behind an alehouse.

Gripping the back of her waistcoat, he hauled her to a stop. She screeched like an angry pig and kicked at his shins. Harry dodged those quick little feet, protesting, "Maela! It is I, Harry!"

"Leave me! Unhand me!" she screamed, flailing with every limb. A bulge in the front of her waistcoat told Harry where the peach had been secreted.

Hearing the genuine panic in her voice, Harry obeyed. She flopped ungracefully upon the dirty stones and stared up at him, eyes furtive, hooded. It was then that Harry noticed: her embroidered emerald green kirtle and waistcoat were new. She looked older, somehow, yet the clean garments emphasized her unwashed condition.

Pushing with both feet, she tried to sidle away, but Harry stepped on the edge of her kirtle and planted his fists upon his hips. He was about to berate the little thief, but something in her dilated eyes stopped him.

He dropped slowly to his knees at her side. "Little maid, I would not harm thee! Have you forgotten your friend so soon?"

Her lips pressed together in an angry line. "If you were my friend, you would free me."

"Maela!" Words seemed to choke him. Questions filled his mind, yet he could voice none of them coherently. "I beheld gentry in the village. . .Art thou at market with. . . ? Thy raiment is new. . ."

Her expression grew darker still.

Frustrated with himself, Harry blurted, "Maela, I have missed thy presence. Thou hast become. . .dear to me, as a sister. I pray for thee daily."

Those haunted eyes widened. "Verily?"

Harry wanted to touch her, but he knew better. In her present state she would inevitably misread his intentions. Words alone must suffice to convince her of his sincerity—but Harry, glib, loquacious Harry, could think of nothing to say. So, right then and there he prayed for his little friend. "Lord Jesus, I ask Thee to calm Maela's heart and teach her to trust Thee and me."

Now her eyes were so wide, he could see his reflection in them. "Does He hear thee?" she whispered. Harry could not catch her voice over the market clamor, but he read her lips and nodded with a smile.

"I would give thee aid, Maela. Confide in me?"

Hope flickered across her face, then faded. She sat up,

scooting away from him. "You can do nothing for me. I am cursed from my birth."

"Not so!" Harry blurted without thinking. "Thou art blessed indeed!"

She made a disrespectful face. "How so?"

"The King of kings would adopt thee for His child! What greater blessing can exist?"

The disgust in her expression brought blood to his face, but he persisted. "If you need aid of any kind, come to me without delay."

She looked him through and through. A little nod, and she scrambled up and out of his reach. Harry's last glimpse was of twinkling bare feet amid rampant petticoats. Another moment and she was lost in the milling crowds.

෨

"Wench, more wine!" a slurred voice commanded.

Maela grimaced, but could only obey. Defying her father was useless—and painful. She had discovered that fact long ago. Hefting the pitcher of red wine, she reentered the great hall and filled cups around the head table.

It was a strange scene. An immense log burned upon the hearth and wax candles lighted the table, yet darkness seemed to hover just above the heads of the diners. Incongruous in the medieval hall were Sir Hanover and his debauched companions, clad though they were in jeweled silks and velvets. In Maela's opinion, they desecrated her castle's venerable stones. True knights had supped at these very tables, great men of old. The castle's time had passed long years ago. Could these men not leave it to crumble in peace?

"Cease thy gaping and come hither, Ishy."

Maela obeyed reluctantly.

"Hold up your head, filthy rag. Almost I shudder to call you mine, for you smell like unto a hog, yet you have your mother's features. Someday shall you mirror her form." Sir Hanover ran his big hands over Maela as he spoke, as though he were pointing out the finer points of a horse. She closed her eyes and tried to distance herself.

"Her music is pleasant to mine ear, Hanover. Entreat her to play another madrigal for us." A younger man with a golden beard seemed kinder than the rest.

"Nay, I have heard enough of her playing. What is the wench's present age?"

Maela quailed at the sound of that deep voice. More than anything in life, she feared Bishop Carmichael.

"Thirteen years, Titus. Thy wait is nigh its end, surely. The child must ripen soon."

Maela gave her father a puzzled glance. "Am I a peach or plum?" she blurted without thinking.

"Silence, wench! You forget yourself." Trenton clouted her across the mouth. His frown cleared as he caught the joke. "My prize peach." The other men began to chuckle in lewd amusement.

"Indeed, a peach for my plucking," the bishop remarked, and the laughter faded. "I hope she will be worth the wait, for thy sake, Hanover. I have no liking for childer and their prattle. The wench is quiet enough, but I would have more flesh and less bone. She must eat more ere I pay thy desired price."

"I shall have words with her keeper. In the interim, Ishy, our vessels are empty once again."

This time when Maela made the rounds with her pitcher, the blond gentleman leaned close and whispered, "I like childer, Ishy."

For a moment she believed him her friend, but then his hand slid around her waist in a distressingly familiar way. Blue eyes glittered as he moistened his red lips and tried to pull her down for a kiss.

Maela cried out, struggling to escape his degrading clutches.

In an instant, a sword point glittered at the blond man's throat. Bishop Carmichael's black eyes held the promise of death.

"Clayton, have done. Bruise not the bishop's peach before its time," Sir Hanover attempted to defuse the situation. His slurred words were jovial, but the warning was real.

"Verily," another man jibed, "bruised peaches are of little worth."

The bishop's long fingers bit into Maela's shoulder as he hauled her out of Clayton's reach. Without another glance, he sheathed his sword and drained his tankard.

It was nearly dawn before the last of Sir Hanover's guests passed out snoring beneath the table. Their servants were likewise prostrate in the kitchen. Maela slid from her hiding place behind a fly-bitten tapestry and crept upstairs to her chamber. There she wrapped a few possessions in a frayed pinafore. Sneaking back downstairs, she tiptoed past the snoring servants and let herself out by the kitchen door.

This time she dared not ride Pegasus. Someone would be certain to notice the pony's absence, and he would be easy to trace. It was a long, hard walk to Harry's cottage, but Maela was desperate.

A few tears escaped as she walked. Many times in the past she had believed that life was not worth living, but never before had she felt this low. In her father's eyes, she was no better than a beast, to be sold out of hand. Since her mother's death, Harry alone had shown Maela kindness and respect.

But Harry was a man. Instinctively, Maela distrusted men even while she yearned for a man's love. If Harry, her only friend, were to prove false. . .it was unthinkable. The memory of his kind eyes and voice had comforted her during many a dark hour since their first meeting.

Jesus. Harry's goodness came from Jesus. Maela spoke the name aloud, savoring its taste upon her lips. "Jesus. Jesus, I beg Thee to save me from this evil."

A Presence filled the emptiness surrounding her. She was no longer alone, yet she did not fear. This unseen Presence was the goodness she sensed whenever Harry was near. Jesus had heard, understood, and answered her desperate plea. Maela's heart pounded; a sense of awe filled her soul.

Maela almost did not recognize Harry's cottage. It was lime-washed, patched, and repaired, and a flintstone chimney emerged from its fresh thatching. Genuine glass window-panes sparkled in the morning light. The yard was neatly cleared, its fences solid. A new jakes had been built beside the livestock shed, with a chicken coop in between.

Before Maela could knock, the door opened and two dogs rushed upon her, whimpering for joy. Harry stood in the doorway, blinking and tousled, wearing only his nightshirt and trunk hose. Patting the excited dogs, Maela tried to explain, "I. . .I had need. . ."

Her face felt hot. She hadn't, somehow, expected to surprise Harry. His nightshirt was unlaced, showing pale skin with a sprinkling of dark hair to match his adolescent beard. His feet and lower legs were bare.

"Down, Laitha, Ragwort," Harry commanded, his voice gruff with sleep. "Enter, child, and welcome."

It was her first glimpse inside. She dropped a small bundle upon the bench beside the door and turned to face him. "Thy cottage is changed indeed. You have labored quickly."

"I had hoped you would approve." Harry indicated the neat stone fireplace set into one wall, the new wooden floor, and lime-washed walls. "I did all but the roof. Sir David's thatcher obliged me there."

"It is fine work."

An awkward silence. Maela glanced around. Harry had acquired a feather bolster. It lay upon the floor in one corner, still rumpled.

"The dogs told me of thine approach. I fear that I am ill-equipped to entertain at this hour. Is Pegasus in the paddock?"

"Nay, I did walk." Her throat felt tight. "I have come to thee, as thou bidst me."

She saw Harry's eyes lower to her feet. "Wherefore, Maela?"

She tried to speak, but could not.

Harry's arm lifted as though he would embrace her, then dropped. "Come, allow me to tend thy feet."

Maela obediently sat upon the bench and let him examine her feet. To her surprise, they were cut and bleeding. Dark stains marked the place where she had been standing on Harry's new floor.

"I shall cleanse them," he told her. "Sit still."

Silently she watched him build up the fire, fetch water from the cistern, and heat it in a kettle. Harry talked to her while he worked, about Lord Marston's new stallion, the dormouse that had built its nest in Samson's manger where Ragwort could not get at it, and his suspicion that Laitha was carrying pups by one of Marston's hounds.

Then he knelt before her and lifted her feet into a basin of warm water. The cuts stung, but Harry's touch sent thrills up her legs as he gently scrubbed her feet and ankles with soft soap and a cloth. The sensation was unlike anything in her previous experience.

"Tell me, Maela, why you have come to me." He patted her feet dry with a clean cloth. They looked strangely white. She was glad the nails were trimmed, at least.

Still kneeling, he looked up at her expectantly. Her memories returned with an unwelcome rush.

"Sir Hanover," she gulped and began again. "Sir Hanover plans to sell me to Bishop Carmichael. They spoke of me as a fruit that must ripen ere it is plucked. I comprehend this not. I do know that I am a slave, Harry—yet I am his child! How can this be?"

Harry swallowed hard, but she was not finished. "Sir Clayton DuBarry grasped me while I waited upon him. He said that he likes childer, but he intended evil. The bishop and Sir Hanover warned him away. I am to belong to the bishop when I am older; therefore, I must not be harmed. I cannot understand, yet I fear men; they are wicked!"

"God save thee, child!" Harry blurted, shaking his head.

Maela's hand pressed against her chest. "In the market you did speak a prayer. God has answered, for I trust thee, and I trust Jesus. I would abide with thee until Sir Hanover departs, two days hence."

It took a moment for her meaning to penetrate. "Here? With me?"

Maela saw varied emotions cross his face: embarrassment, suspicion, pity, doubt.

"You fled from me at the market, and today you entrust your life into my keeping?"

It did seem strange, she had to admit. "I do. I trust thee."

"But can I trust thee?"

She caught his meaning and flushed. "I would not steal, Harry. I know it is wrong. It. . .is no habit of mine."

"I paid the grocer for the fruit."

Maela felt dreadful. "Why?"

He rose abruptly, throwing his hands up. "I would not have thee lose thy hand as a thief! Maela, will not thy father seek thee?"

Her head bowed. "He will seek me not here."

"Had I an alternative, I would avail myself of it," Harry muttered. "But as yet I know not any brethren in this county. Yea, child, you may remain here with me."

Her face began to glow with delight. "I could go in disguise as a lad. Have you a spare jerkin and hose to lend me?"

He frowned. "Nay. Thou art a lady, and I would have thee remain so."

She sighed in resignation. "Would that I were a lad and could wear trunk hose. 'Twould simplify tree-climbing."

Harry answered in a matter-of-fact voice. "You should wear drawers beneath thy kirtle. My sisters and mother do wear them."

"Indeed? They do wear drawers?" Maela's delight was evident.

" 'Tis the Italian style. My mother would ne'er adopt a scandalous fashion, but drawers are modest and sensible." Harry's face looked flushed. Speaking of drawers must be difficult for him, Maela concluded.

After they had broken their fast with toasted bread and cheese, Harry warned Maela to remain indoors while he was away. She was not to care for the outdoor animals in his absence, but she was free to amuse herself indoors with the dogs. She promised obedience, feeling somewhat frightened.

"I shall return as early as possible," he assured her. "God be with thee."

All seemed normal at Marston Hall that day, until Harry entered the house to take measurements. Several gentlemen stood in a semicircle about the finished portion of Harry's carved screen.

". . .and but look at the rose petals. Are they not lifelike? And they of solid walnut!" Sir David Marston was saying.

Eyes widening, Harry turned to sneak away.

"Ah, and here is the artisan in the flesh. Joiner, I would speak with thee. Tarry if thou wilt, and come hither to greet my guests."

Harry squared his shoulders and turned. *Help me, Lord!*

The gentlemen regarded Harry with a mixture of interest and disdain. "Sir Hanover Trenton, Bishop Titus Carmichael, Sir Clayton DuBarry, and the Hon. Samuel Fredericks, meet Harold Jameson, joiner."

Only Fredericks showed interest. "Indeed? Well, joiner, I must express myself enamored of thy work. Would you take employ at my house near Norwich? Of a certain, I shall wait patiently until Marston's screen is complete," he added with a chuckle.

"But he shall have more projects when this screen is complete!" Marston protested. "Many days have I pondered the south stairs, and have come at last to a decision. I would have dragons, or perhaps lions, mounted upon the posts at its base. And again, the great hall has need of a surround for the fireplace, something magnificent in walnut, I believe. Would you create this masterpiece for me when the screen is complete, Harry, my boy?"

Harry felt awkward, but he agreed to stay on.

The other gentlemen looked askance at Marston's friendliness toward Harry. Such camaraderie from a member of the gentry toward an artisan was rare indeed, but then Sir David's knighthood was of recent origin. Although Lord Marston was not extremely wealthy, the high-quality Norfolk sheep's wool produced on his farms sold for peak prices in nearby market towns, and he could afford to gradually decorate his new house with beautiful things. He was a kindly, jolly man who loved his wife, son, and three daughters and treated his tenants fairly. Harry liked him.

"This talk is all well and good," Sir Hanover interrupted

gruffly, "but it answers not my purpose." He turned to Harry and pinned him with a stare. "Have you seen a small damsel about the manor? She is a slave, gone missing from the castle."

"I will look for such a damsel, sir," Harry bowed slightly.

"Repeat this to other servants, for I would have her returned promptly."

Harry nodded his understanding, but made no promises he could not honor. He carefully kept all emotion from his expression, and the men noticed nothing amiss.

Sir Hanover was not a tall man, but he was trim and strong, with auburn hair, mustache, and pointed beard. His plumed velvet hat, embroidered silk jerkin with shoulder picadils, puffed trunks, trunk hose, and nether hose looked ridiculous in Harry's eyes, but he knew this attire was the height of fashion.

The other men were similarly attired, though perhaps with fewer jewels. Bishop Carmichael wore nothing but black, though his clothing was ornate in style. He was evidently a secular bishop—appointed his position and property as a reward for service to the queen. On the whole he was not an ill-favored man, yet the idea of his owning little Maela caused Harry's big fists to clench.

At last Harry was dismissed. The other men watched him depart—sans measurements. He would come back for them later.

"An outsize lout, is he not?" DuBarry sneered.

"I'd give a thousand quid to have such shoulders," Fredericks remarked wistfully.

Then the door closed, and Harry heard no more.

Her respite was over. All her life she would treasure the memory of two blessed days in Harry's cottage. Harry had treated her like a queen, serving her meals, attending to her every word and need, reading her Bible stories until late in the night. He had even given her his bed while he slept in the shed with Samson and Genevieve. She had never before experienced such luxury as that feather bolster.

But now Sir Hanover had gone away, and she must return to her prison. Before Harry arrived home from work, Maela gathered her few possessions, hugged the dogs in farewell, donned her soft new leather shoes, and walked home through field and forest. Tears streaked her cheeks and dripped upon her waistcoat. Already she missed Harry dreadfully, but she simply could not have bidden him farewell without crying. Maela hated to cry in public.

Her footsteps slowed as she approached Castle Trent. She stopped, trembling, beside the ruined gatehouse. At times she loved her castle, but now the crumbling keep seemed to loom over her like a malevolent entity. Black clouds roiled across the sky behind it. Thunder rumbled in the distance, startling Maela back into motion. She darted across the courtyard and pushed at the kitchen door.

Castle Trent had been modified during her grandfather's tenure. A wing had been added, connecting the kitchen with the keep. Sir Oliver Blickney Trenton had discounted the increased possibility of fire spreading to the living area, for modern fireplaces and ovens were much safer than the open cooking fires of earlier days, and besides, his castle had been modified structurally to withstand fire. Sir Oliver had proved more lucky than accurate, for during Sir Hanover's boyhood, a fire had, in fact, destroyed the upper bailey, though the castle's main living areas escaped harm. Maela's grandmother spent most of her time in the kitchen and scullery. Maela spent much of her time alone in the cavernous keep.

The kitchen door opened easily beneath her hand, and her hopes rose. She slid along the kitchen wall, her eyes fastened to the motionless form slumped over one filthy table. Perhaps she would not have to explain her absence at all! Perhaps her grandmother would pass off her escape as a harmless escapade and—

The slumped figure suddenly lunged into motion and gnarled fingers gripped Maela's upper arm. "Where have you been, malapert knave? Thy sire did hunt for thee high and low, Ishy, and did blame thy grandmother for thine absence! Thy grandmother, who tends thee as a ewe lamb! Doltish lout of a wench! Did you think to escape my wrath?"

Maela writhed in her grandmother's grasp, to no avail. A

horny fist clouted her upon the side of the head, making her ears ring. "This for my trouble, thou lousy lurdan! And this!" Repeatedly she slapped Maela's cheeks, ignoring her cries for mercy.

"Out upon thee now, and should you sneak away again, I shall give thee to Dob and let him punish thee, errant wench!" Breathing hard, Hera released the child and sank back upon the bench.

Maela scurried from the kitchen, along a passageway, through an empty chamber, up spiral stairs, and along a gallery to the dismal comfort of her room. Tonight she would have no candles to relieve its stygian darkness. Shivering with shock and fear, she dropped upon her lumpy bed and heaved with dry sobs. "Where art Thou, God?" she whimpered. "Why didst Thou not protect me from Grandmere?"

The door slammed against the wall, and Dobbin Titwhistle entered the kitchen. He loomed over Hera Coats, slapping a crop against his heavy boots. "Up, thou drunken witch. What aroused thy wrath? Has the wench returned?"

"Yea, and I have punished her," Hera snarled, pouring another tumbler of port from a flagon.

Dob snatched up the flagon and sniffed it. "I heard the master say that the port was low, and now I find thee here soaking in it. What sayest thou, witch?"

"I have earned it, as you have earned the rent you hold back from Sir Hanover," she mocked. "Threaten me not, fool. A pox upon thee!"

Thunder rumbled outside, nearer this time.

Dob paled. "Repeal thy curse, woman, I beg of thee."

"For the present," she relented, grinning widely. The woman still possessed all of her teeth—an almost unheard-of feat at her age. Only a witch could have managed it, the townsfolk said.

"Where is the wench? I would have words with her," Dob explained more respectfully, flourishing the switch. His heavy brows drew together. "The master did lay her escape at my door!"

"No more than at mine," the old woman growled. "She is in her chamber." In spite of the whip, Hera did not believe he would harm the child, so she allowed him to pass. Sir Hanover had made it clear to all that the girl was not to be tampered with.

Hera dozed again until a flash of lightning roused her. Faint screams reached her ears just before thunder rolled over the castle. Hera bolted to her feet, blinking in surprise.

"The fool!" she exclaimed, along with more potent adjectives. Grabbing a poker from the fire, she hurried to the spiral staircase and laboriously made her way to Maela's chamber. Sounds of blows and cries of pain fanned her wrath. Opening the door, which fortunately Dob had failed to latch, she entered, brandishing the poker.

"Unhand her," she croaked. Dob turned to face her, saw the glowing poker, and froze. His grip on Maela's arm relaxed.

Maela scurried past her grandmother and crouched against the gallery wall. Her new clothing was shredded. Throbbing weals rose upon her back and legs; oozing blood stuck to her smock.

"You well know Sir Hanover's decree concerning the wench," Hera stated in her creaking voice. "Yet you would disregard it for a moment's pleasure! Thou art the doltish lout, Dob! This day I do place a curse upon Castle Trent: Any man that enters herein before Sir Hanover's return shall be carried away by the devil himself!"

A flash lit the room in blinding white light with a crash that shook the castle to its foundations. The sudden roar of pouring rain on slate and lead sheet roofing filled their ears.

Dob's eyes widened until the whites showed all the way around. With a fearful screech he rushed out the door, crashed into the gallery railing, passed Maela without seeing her, and thundered down the stairs. The front door slammed behind him with a force that echoed throughout the stone keep.

Cackling in delighted triumph, Hera Coats swept past her shivering granddaughter and slowly descended the stairs.

# *five*

*Likewise, I say unto you, there is joy in the presence of the angels of God over one sinner that repenteth.*
Luke 15:10

Four days later, Maela had healed enough to ride to Harry's cottage for an evening. Upon her arrival she saw Harry's reaction to her battered face, but he seemed to accept her explanation that she had fallen. Once she saw him perusing the fading bruises on her bare forearms and the patches on her new garments, but he said nothing. She did not stay long, neither would she sit down, but her eyes followed Harry's every move as though his presence sustained her life.

The bruises eventually faded, the stripes healed, and no further beatings ensued. Dob left Maela strictly alone, and her grandmother virtually ignored her. Sir Hanover did not return, and the bishop neglected Trenton parish.

Maela had ways of discovering how long Dob would be away from the castle each day. She had memorized his routine, and easily caught any variation from his usual behavior patterns. On most days she could find an hour or two to spend at Harry's cottage, though not always while he was at home. Friday was the best day of the week, for Dob left the castle grounds early, visited every alehouse in the village, and generally did not return until morning.

Upon her arrival, Maela would free the chickens, feed the animals, brush Samson and Pegasus, pet Genevieve's twin buck kids, and play with the dogs while Harry worked around the cottage.

That first summer, Harry transplanted wild rosebushes to frame the front door, and Maela tended them lovingly until they adjusted to the change. "Imagine them in bloom," she murmured, smoothing a glossy leaf with one finger. To please her, Harry bartered for bedding plants with the gardener at the manor, acquiring perennial vines and shrubs in exchange for carved knickknacks. Before long, her flower garden nearly equaled Harry's kitchen garden in size and effort expended.

When inclement weather prevented outdoor labor, Harry built furniture: an oak table and benches, two armchairs, a bedstead for his feather bolster, a wardrobe and washstand. No cottage in the county boasted finer furniture, though it was rather crowded.

Not all of Harry's free time was devoted to the cottage. With Sir David's permission he took Maela fishing on manor grounds, teaching her to construct a pole and line, dig bait, and prepare the fish once caught. Her acuity and aptitude prompted him to try new lessons; one thing led to another, and Harry soon found himself in the role of tutor. Ishmaela seemed determined to extract every drop of knowledge and skill from his brain, and Harry thoroughly enjoyed teaching her.

Once introduced to kitchen arts, Maela was enthralled with cookery. Harry taught her the basic skills and recipes he had learned from his mother. Maela mastered them, then branched out on her own. Many of her attempts were dismal failures, but the dogs enjoyed them. Harry tasted every experiment, though he might have wished that the hands kneading the bread dough and chopping the produce were cleaner—Maela still resisted his attempts to introduce her to hygiene.

The joy of learning was addictive, and Maela delighted her tutor with her rapid progress. Harry used his Bible as a primer, and Maela produced a treasure trove of writing materials from the castle: quills, ink, parchment, paper, pencils, slates, and chalk. Along with reading and writing, Harry taught mathematics, Latin, history, and music.

Best of all was Scripture reading time. Maela soaked up knowledge of Jesus with every fiber of her being, begging Harry for more each day. He introduced her to Adam and

Eve, Abraham, Moses, Joshua, Ruth, David—her interest was unquenchable.

Maela designed drawers for herself out of her mother's old flannel petticoat. They were both comfortable and convenient. Modesty had been a foreign concept to her, but now Maela did concern herself with it, since modesty concerned Harry, and apparently it concerned God.

One day in early December, Laitha's pups arrived. When Harry returned home from work one evening, he found the mother and nine pups settled, not in the whelping box he had provided, but in his best blanket at the foot of the bed. The blanket was ruined, of course, but he could not be angry with the new mother—Laitha's manifest contentment touched his heart. He gently moved the family to their cozy box, and the new mother reluctantly accepted the change.

Ragwort was confused. His best friend would have nothing to do with him; she snarled when he so much as approached her nest. He felt better once Harry sat down and let him hop into his lap. Harry tipped his chair back on two legs and scratched the terrier's belly. "We shall have little attention from our womenfolk these days, Rag. The pups shall receive all their love, I fear."

Harry ate a cold supper, assuming Maela would not come that night, for it was snowing and windy. But commotion outside warned him of company. Ragwort stared at the crack beneath the door, his tail quivering. Harry opened the door, and Maela stumbled inside. He caught her, staring aghast at her blue lips and frosty eyelashes. Only a threadbare shawl draped her head and shoulders. Her hands were like blocks of ice.

"Pegasus is stabled." She gave Harry a sheepish smile before seeking out Laitha's box. "The pups are whelped! I knew it! Oh, Laitha!"

Harry released her to run to the puppies. She must not be quite frozen, after all. Words of reprimand died upon his lips. She had taken a terrible chance, all for the sake of Laitha's pups.

To Harry's surprise, Laitha made no demur when Maela picked up her puppies and admired each one. The dog had seemed uneasy when he handled them. "Six males and three females. A magnificent family, indeed!"

"The sire is Sir David's prize staghound. These pups shall be valuable."

"They are already valuable to me. Oh, Harry, behold this tiny face!"

Laitha licked the pup along with Maela's fingers. She seemed delighted with the girl's attention.

"What is Ragwort's opinion of them?" Maela glanced back at the scruffy terrier.

"Not high, I fear. They are not his, of course; he is too small. However, there is a litter of terriers at the manor that bears his likeness. Lyttleton declares the pups are Ragwort's."

"Shall you take one?"

"I possess eleven dogs at present. I have no need of more!"

While Maela petted Laitha and cheered Ragwort by playing tug-o-war, Harry balanced on two back chair legs and his toes, his hands busy with a small carving. The growls and giggles ceased, and Maela reclined before the fire. Harry was relieved to see that color and warmth had returned to her face and hands.

Maela turned her head and stated bluntly, "Harry, I must tell you that I am now a disciple of Jesus Christ."

Harry blinked. "I thought you had decided this long ago."

"Nay. I loved Jesus and wanted to learn more of Him, but I did not wish to repent of my sins. Now I have done so, and He has forgiven me. My life is now His."

She spoke firmly, but Harry heard a little tremor at the end. His hands fell to his lap; his front chair legs hit the floor. "This is a vital decision, Ishmaela. Never shalt thou make a greater." A smile lifted his mustache. "Well done. The angels are rejoicing with thee, as I am also."

Ishmaela nodded. Her eyes returned to the fire. "Does this mean that God has adopted me into His family?"

Harry wondered at the intensity of the question. "Indeed, it does. Thou art His child and my sister in Christ Jesus."

"You have read to me of Abraham, Isaac, and Ishmael. I had never heard the story."

She fell silent. "And?" Harry prompted after a long pause.

"I understand much now. . .about my mother, and. . .my name." She rolled over and looked directly at Harry. "I was not the child of promise, Harry."

"Not in man's eyes, perhaps, but in God's eyes thou art of infinite value. Jesus laid down his life for thee, Maela. There can be no greater love than this."

She stared into his eyes as though reading his very soul. Harry said softly, "His Word is sure, Maela. You are a child of His promises, and He never fails to keep His Word."

Silence fell. The gammon Harry had spitted over the fire dripped and crackled. He pulled it out and placed it on a plate for the girl, along with a roll and an apple. "Eat well, Maela."

She accepted the food, munching quietly, her thoughts far away.

"You have added flesh to your bones since spring. Thou art slender as a birch sapling, but a breath of wind can no longer bear thee away."

Maela smiled self-consciously, still chewing. She swallowed and vouchsafed, "You have fattened me well, Harry. 'Tis your provender which sustains me. Now, I must return to the castle, for Dob took the cob Orwell to ride this day, which means he shall not stay away long."

As she rose, Harry produced from his wardrobe a woolen cloak and rabbit fur muff. "I had intended these for Christmas, but you have need of them now."

"Oh! Oh, Harry!" Maela clasped his gifts in her arms and buried her face in the fur.

"May I walk thee home?"

Recovering, she shook her head and donned the cloak. It covered her slight figure from head to toe. "It is most wondrous warm. I shall depart now. Tend those pups with care!"

❧

Sliding between mossy stones, Maela hunkered down to survey the castle grounds. In winter her natural cover was sparse, consisting only of dry grasses, bare trees, and a few clumps of gorse. It was not yet noon, but Dob and the other retainers had left early to join holiday celebrations at the local bear garden and pubs. Grandmere had retired to her chambers with a large pitcher of spirits, leaving Maela free to celebrate Christmas as she pleased.

Maela scampered into the forest, taking her roundabout path to Pegasus's snowy, overgrazed pasture. The pony greeted her with his cheerful nicker. "Soon thou shalt enjoy a full manger, my friend," she assured him, hopping upon his back. The sturdy pony seemed to have shrunk somewhat during the last year, but he still carried his mistress easily.

"Welcome! 'Glory to God in the highest, and on earth, peace, good will toward men,' " Harry called, rising politely as Maela stepped through the door. He had been ladling juices over a roasting fowl and turning the spit.

"Let us rejoice and be glad," Maela agreed. " 'For unto us a child is born.' " Harry's joy was contagious. Contentment flooded her heart. She dropped a package on the bench and pulled off her oversized boots and new cloak.

Ragwort sat on the hearth with his eyes glued to the dripping bird. Laitha lay in her box while the puppies nursed. She lifted her face to Maela's loving touch, but Ragwort barely acknowledged the girl's presence with a glance and a tail wag.

Maela could not blame him. The aroma was mouth-watering. Then an unwelcome thought struck her. "That is not one of our hens?"

Harry chuckled and hunkered back down on his low stool. His legs stuck out at angles like a spider's. "Nay, I would not slay any pet of thine, Ishmaela; I love mine own life too well. The bird was a gift from Sir David—also ham, pastries, and dried figs. Kind in him, was it not? The manor festivities upon Christmas Eve were grand indeed. We did eat our fill, field hands, house servants, and all, and played and danced until our feet ached and our voices failed. I wished for thy presence, Maela."

"I am thankful enough for this day," she replied, peering over his shoulder at the chicken. The fire's heat made her icy cheeks burn. She could imagine Harry dancing and singing with a pretty maid on each arm. The thought gave her no joy.

"I have a gift for thee," Harry said suddenly. "Turn the spit, and I will bring it."

"But my cloak and muff. . .they were my gift," she faltered, though her eyes brightened.

"Nay, 'twas insufficient."

Maela willingly took his place on the stool. Her kirtle settled around her as she bent to her task.

From a cupboard over the washstand, Harry retrieved his gift. Holding it behind his back, he approached her. Firelight twinkled in his brown eyes. Squatting beside her, he held out the gift on one callused hand.

It was the carving he had begun the night of the puppies' birth, a gracefully carved dove. Each delicate feather was carved in detail; the sweetness of the bird's expression brought tears to Maela's eyes. Carefully she lifted it from Harry's hand, her thin fingers trembling. "It is the most beautiful thing. . .its breast looks to be downy soft, though it is of wood." The polished wood glowed in the firelight as she pressed the bird to her cheek and closed her eyes.

"It pleases thee?" A redundant question.

Leaning over, Maela squeezed his neck with one skinny arm. "It pleases me." He looked satisfied.

Leaving Harry to turn the spit, she retrieved her bundle and placed it at his feet. "For thee." She stepped back, hands clasped behind her back.

"I must rescue our supper first." Harry removed the chicken from the spit and set it upon a platter to cool—out of Ragwort's reach. The dog transferred his fixed gaze to the table.

Then, folding back the corners of a grayed and stained pinafore, Harry uncovered the gift, a needleworked pillow. He smiled in recognition. "It is Laitha and Ragwort. Smells of flowers."

"I did stuff it with lavender," she informed him eagerly.

A crude yet artful representation of the two dogs at play in a field of wildflowers decorated the canvas rectangle. Such detailed needlework must have required many hours of painstaking labor. Harry traced Laitha's curved crewel spine with one rough finger, then Ragwort's face. She had somehow captured Laitha's air of tragedy and the terrier's saucy, scruffy appeal.

Maela saw him bite his lip. Leaning back on his stool, he stared at the thatching overhead, fighting to control his emotions. His Adam's apple bobbed up and down beneath his beard, and a pulse throbbed in the hollow of his brown throat. Maela wanted to climb into his lap and snuggle against his chest as Ragwort sometimes did; instead she simply watched him with tender eyes. Her bird was lovely, but Harry was the most beautiful creature she had ever seen.

"It is fine indeed. Nothing could please me more," he finally croaked, rubbing his eyes with his thumb and fingers. He turned to finish preparing the meal, keeping the pillow tucked under one elbow. "We shall starve while I forget my business here," he rumbled.

Maela caressed her dove, satisfied that Harry's reaction had been worth every stabbed finger, every ripped-out stitch. Her mother's training, not to mention her mother's supply of yarns and needles, had finally been of some use.

After a most satisfying feast, they settled around the fire. For once, Harry was not carving. He rubbed Ragwort's back, staring into the fire. The little dog's belly was tightly rounded. He sighed contentedly in his sleep, sprawled across Harry's lap. For a while, Maela sat beside Laitha's box, fondling and crooning to each puppy in turn. Then she scooted closer to the fire, closer to Harry, sitting tailor-fashion.

"Tell me of thy mother," Harry demanded suddenly.

"Mother had golden hair and blue, blue eyes and white, soft skin. She taught me to dance and ride and stitch fancywork. She wore colorful gowns that flowed about her when she danced. . .I was eight years of age when Mother fell ill of a fever and died in the night." Maela's low voice faded away.

Suddenly sitting up straighter, she proclaimed, "Grandmere loves me not. She has eyes that. . .I cannot explain. She has cast a spell upon the castle."

Harry's brows lowered. "Maela, surely you do not fear such things."

"Nay, but Dob does. Grandmere's witchery has helped me in this way."

"What do you mean?"

"Once last summer Dob was. . .cruel to me. Grandmere laid a spell around the castle, cursing any man that entered the keep ere its master's return. Since that time, Dob has troubled me not."

Muscles worked in Harry's jaw, making his beard twitch. Maela wondered what he was thinking.

"How do you manage to escape the keep without their knowledge?"

Maela's shoulders jerked. Just above a whisper she replied, "A secret tunnel."

"A secret tunnel," Harry mused softly. "I have heard of such things concerning these castles. How did you discover its existence?"

"I found it while playing. I doubt anyone living knows of it, save me. My one fear is that someday Dob will notice Pegasus missing and discover my secrets. Grandmere suffers pain in her limbs and drinks to excess. Because she never climbs the spiral staircase to my chamber without dire need, she knows not of mine absences. This morn she started early upon a large jug of rum; therefore I left earlier than my wont."

"Does she beat you?" Harry asked quietly.

Maela felt warm. She turned away from the fire, away from Harry. "Not often. She threatens horrors beyond imagining should her commands be disobeyed. I know Jesus will protect me from her evil spells; nevertheless, I dare not cross Grandmere without desperate need. She has excellent aim with a skillet."

"And does she work about the castle? Cleaning, baking, washing, and such?"

"She collects and dries herbs for her potions, and prepares food for herself and for me. Dob and his like fare for themselves. I know not how. There is provender enough, but

Grandmere does not trouble herself to prepare it properly, and she allows me not to try my hand. If you did not share of your bounty, I was like to have died of hunger long ago. Cleanliness is unknown to Grandmere. The bowls and suchlike are scoured with sand ere we eat. That is all. Once I swept out the old rush matting as you have taught me, then sprinkled fresh rushes and herbs about. Grandmere was asleep, and I do not believe she noticed my handiwork when she awoke. I try to make things finer, but there is little to work with."

Maela looked troubled by her ineptitude, but Harry was touched by her efforts. "Make no excuse for thy labors; they are worthy. I might come to the castle and help thee. Often I behold its tower above the treetops and think of thee hidden within. 'Tis no proper place for a child. Mayhap I could reason with thy grandmother—"

"Nay! It can never be. I must depart. All thanks for my dove and for the bountiful feast." Frightened, Maela leaped to her feet and began to don the large boots she had scavenged from a bedchamber in the castle.

Looking startled and rather hurt, Harry held her cloak then tried to open the door, but she ignored his good manners and let herself out. The two dogs followed her, but turned back quickly. Daylight had gone, leaving frigid darkness, though it was not yet five hours past noon. A thick fog rose from the melting snow. Maela could scarcely see to the shed where Pegasus waited.

The pony was not thrilled to see her, but he made no protest when she led him outside and climbed upon his back. When she rode past the cottage, she was surprised to see Harry in the doorway, silhouetted against the fire. "God be with thee," Maela called.

"Fare thee well, Maela," Harry called back. He sounded strangely forlorn.

## six

*The Lord is my light and my salvation; whom shall I fear?*
*the Lord is the strength of my life; of whom shall I be afraid?*
*When the wicked, even mine enemies and my foes,*
*came upon me. . .they stumbled and fell.*
Psalm 27:1–2

A few weeks later Ishmaela did not show up at the cottage for several days in a row. Harry philosophically accepted the first few days of her absence, for sleety snow driven before a knife-edged wind would keep most people indoors—though Maela was unlike most people. Laitha's bright-eyed, tumbling, fuzzy puppies were an irresistible lure to the girl. It was strange, indeed, that she did not come.

After six days of lonely, worried waiting, he could bear it no longer and prepared a sack of food and herbs. He let the dogs out, then shut them back into the house and set out toward the castle. Anything might have happened to the child. She could be sick or injured or imprisoned. . .

"It had best not be Dobbin Titwhistle," he muttered grimly. He had seen Dob about town, a burly man with florid face, bushy beard, and a large belly. The thought of the man harming Maela made Harry's protective instincts rise in full force.

"Wish I had a horse." Not for the first time, he imagined himself riding up to the castle gates and demanding entrance, then galloping away with Maela across his saddle. His daydream always degenerated into the more realistic prospect of riding over on Samson, his feet dragging on the ground as they jounced along. He gave a rueful chuckle. "I would find a place as court jester, more like."

He pulled his hood over his face in a vain attempt to shield it from the wind. It was no longer sleeting, but it was dark, with no moon or starlight to brighten his path. Patches of snow remaining beside the way took on a ghostly aspect in Harry's eyes. Wind whipped naked treetops into frenzy. Branches strewed the narrow road, swirling about as the wind caught them. Harry heard and felt a crash somewhere to his left; a mighty tree had fallen before the storm.

He nearly missed the turnoff to Castle Trent, a black tunnel through the trees. A chill caused by neither sleet nor wind trickled down his spine as he entered it. Mocking voices in the wind screamed of doom and disaster. His flesh began to creep; the hair on his scalp lifted.

Harry stopped and closed his eyes. His cloak whipped and fluttered about his legs, but he stood like a rock in the center of the path. "Lord," he spoke aloud. "I ask Thy protection and blessing upon this mission. Uphold Ishmaela with Thine Almighty Hand; keep her safe in Thee. Thou art greater far than any power of darkness and fear, and all creation rests in Thy Hands. Help me to find Thy little child this night, and give Thine angels charge over us. In Jesus' name I ask this."

Shoulders squared, he strode down the path like a conquering hero. His armor was invisible, yet it was invulnerable. Now the wind sounded angry, defiant.

Castle Trent appeared out of the night, seeming to glow with a silvery light against the black sky. There were no castle gates; they had long since crumbled. So much for that fantasy. A moat had once surrounded the grounds; of it, only a grassy depression remained. Inside the moat's outline, piles of rubble overcome by moss, bracken, and brambles were all that was left of the castle walls. Only the tall stone keep and a few outbuildings remained intact. Few of the keep's lower windows showed flickers of light, signs of human life.

Harry paused beside the ruined gatehouse, sensing danger. His eyes darted from corner to dark corner, suspecting. . . he knew not what. One hand on his knife sheath, he walked into the courtyard where knights had gathered for battle one hundred years before. Almost he could hear their shouts, the clatter of hooves and clink of armor.

Nay, that metallic clank was of the present. . .

Harry sprang to one side just as a pike pierced the air where he had been standing. His cloak billowed around him; there was a sound of rending fabric as the pike ripped it from his back.

Carried by the momentum of the thrust, a large body stumbled past, uttering a frustrated oath. Harry grasped the man by the back of his jerkin, hauled him off his feet, and kicked the cloaked pike out of reach. Whipping out his hunting knife, he held it to the man's throat from behind, pressing its edge into the skin until a trickle of blood emerged. "Hold," he ordered, as though his captive could do otherwise.

Wheeling to look for other assailants, Harry held the man before him like a shield. The courtyard was empty.

"Slay me not!" the man begged through clenched teeth. "Who art thou?"

"One full willing to dispatch cowardly assassins such as you," Harry snarled, fear still whipping the blood through his veins. "Where is the child?"

He felt surprise ripple through the heavy body. "The child?"

"Lord Trenton's daughter."

"He has no daughter," the voice was unconvincing. "If you desire ransom, take the boy child from his home near London. I could counsel thee how to accomplish it."

Harry's teeth clenched. "Foul traitor!"

"Nay, I am faithful to his lordship," Dob whined, ready to butter his bread on either side.

"Less talk of thy worthless loyalty," Harry spoke sharply. "Where is the girl child?"

"In the castle," Dob gasped as the knife pressed harder. "I've done nothing to anger thee, lord."

"But for attempting to skewer me, I trust that is true."

"You should fear the witch Hera. She commands the powers of darkness; indeed, I know it." Genuine fear laced the foreman's gravely voice. "She has placed a curse upon the castle so that no man dare enter until Sir Trenton's return."

"I give thee fair warning, Master Titwhistle," thick sarcasm colored the title of respect, "should any harm come to the damsel, thy life is forfeit. She is under protection far greater than any witch could provide."

"How do you know of the wench? Art thou a wizard?"

"I have means beyond thy ken" was Harry's enigmatic reply. If Dob believed he was a sorcerer, so be it.

Apparently this was exactly the conclusion Dob had arrived at. Who but a sorcerer could know of Sir Hanover's child or dodge a pike thrust with such perfect timing? Dob was no fool, but superstition clouded his judgment. Shaking with fear, he offered no resistance when Harry bound his hands behind his back using his own woolen hose. Rather than leave the helpless man exposed to the elements, Harry locked him into a storeroom, certain that he would be found in the morning. One hazard eliminated.

Harry freed his cloak but left the pike where it lay. The castle loomed above him, ominous, cold. Ishmaela's home? It was difficult to imagine his lively little companion dwelling in this gloomy fortress.

"Lord," he spoke softly while wiping clean his knife's blade. "I thank Thee for Thy protection this night. Hera Coats has allied herself with Thy sworn enemies, and will doubtless strive to prevent mine entry. I ask Thee in Jesus' name to defeat Thine enemies and allow Thy servant free access to Castle Trent."

With a raucous cackling and clatter of wings, a flock of rooks launched from the castle battlements, circled once, then headed north above the treetops, a ragged black cloud, tattered by the wind. Harry stared up into the darkness, hearing the noise, but unable to determine its source.

Taking a deep breath, he shrugged his shoulders to relax them and headed for the keep, knife in hand. This time he kept an eye on his back trail, not caring to be surprised more than once a night.

The drawbridge, rotted and treacherous to unwary feet, lay across the dry inner moat. The portcullis was up, set, and ready to cut off the unwary or unwelcome visitor. Within these barriers, stone stairs led up to an enormous oaken door set deep in the outer wall. It was a far from pleasant prospect. Harry paused at the base of the steps. He could not imagine Maela opening that door. Perhaps there was another.

Circling the base of the rectangular keep, he soon discovered the attached kitchen wing. A light glowed from within. He knocked on the door. No answer. Circling the castle once more, he studied its windows. They were too narrow to enter even if he should manage to climb up.

Returning to the kitchen door, he pushed at its iron ring. The door swung open with a low groan. Slightly rattled by this easy access, he paused in the doorway, brandishing his knife, but nothing happened. A short, narrow hallway lay within, dimly lit by a fire in the room beyond.

Harry stepped inside. There was a weird scream and a scuffle at his feet. With a startled yell, he flourished his knife and crouched in a defensive position—but it was only a cat rushing to escape through the open doorway. He must have trodden upon its tail. From the courtyard it turned to glare at him with glowing eyes and yowled again before gliding into the shadows.

Harry swallowed hard, blinked, let out his breath in a puff, and grinned. "Overmuch talk of witches makes me fear a little cat!"

Flaring coals cast a red glow over the kitchen's tiled floor, filthy worktables, and a jumbled assortment of baskets, barrels, pottery, and cast-iron pots. A heap draped across one of the tables emitted a low rumbling noise. Harry silently moved close enough to recognize a human shape and to understand the significance of the empty jug at its elbow. He gently lifted one of the woman's shoulders, showing a lined, yellowed countenance with slack jaw and deep bags beneath the closed eyes. Greasy, grayish hair slipped from beneath her cap.

"Mistress Hera, I presume," he said and released her. "So much for thine evil spells. Thou hast succumbed to an evil of thine own making." It was difficult to imagine this sot as

Maela's grandmother. Although the woman might have been handsome in her youth, it was impossible to discern beauty in her ravaged face now.

Taking a beeswax candle from the kitchen, Harry began to explore, checking chambers and hallways, softly calling Maela's name. Only scuffling rodents and echoes replied. Mildew and dry rot tickled his nose. He stifled a sneeze, then another. Wind moaned through the windows, lifting tapestries from chamber walls in ghostly waves. Harry's candle flickered wildly. Every sound, every leaping shadow caused his heart to race. Though he felt chilled, sweat beaded his brow. *I wonder*, he thought, *have I covered the ground floor, or have I traveled in circles? Each chamber looks like the one before.*

Near the entry hall he found the stairwell, dark and steep. Holding his long knife in his right hand, the candle in his left, he began to ascend. Eventually, the spiral stairwell opened into a gallery. He extended the candle into it while standing poised on the stairs. Three doors opened into the gallery; all were closed. Opposite the doors, at Harry's left hand, was a waist-high frame barrier, and beyond this barrier a vast, empty space. Casting wary glances over both shoulders and listening with every nerve in his body, he stepped into the gallery. Its wooden floor creaked ominously beneath his feet.

Before trying the doors, he held his candle over the barrier to see what lay beyond. Heavy beams supported a vaulted ceiling. Long tables lay below, lined with heavy chairs and benches. It was the castle's great hall. The gallery overlooked it from on high, a good two stories up. Leaning slightly against the barrier railing, Harry felt it give beneath his hand. Instantly, he backed away, eyes wide. This place requires the services of a good joiner. . .but I shall not apply for the position.

Harry paused before the first door.

"Maela?"

Silence.

He knocked at the next door. "Maela? Can you hear me?"

"Harry?" A guttural reply. It could be no one but Maela, though it sounded nothing like her.

He took a deep breath, gulped, and felt tears prick behind his eyes. His relief was beyond measure. "Maela! Yea, truly 'tis Harry."

The door creaked open to reveal Maela's pallid face. "Harry, thou art in danger here!" she barked, then began to cough.

The sound thrust a knife of fear between Harry's ribs. The candle shook in his hand that had been rock-steady a moment before. "Thou art ill! I did fear it."

Maela shook her head. " 'Tis but a cough. I shall recover. Harry, you must go away! Should Grandmere discover thee, or Master Dob. . ." Her eyes implored him, but he pushed past her into the room, his feet crunching on withered rush matting.

A tiny fire consisting of a few twigs flickered on the hearth but produced no discernible heat. No wonder the child was ill. The dank, dark chamber was perhaps six by eight feet, with a small doorway to the garderobe near the wall. Maela's bed was a straw pallet on the floor. Two moth-eaten blankets and her woolen cloak were its only coverings. From the corner of one eye he saw furtive movement near the hearth—a mouse, no doubt. The entire castle reeked of vermin.

He turned to Maela. Arms wrapped about her body, she shivered, clad in only her shift and red flannel drawers—no nightcap. Tattered sleeves dangled at her elbows. The sagging neckline revealed protruding collarbones. She had lost considerable weight. Dirty ankles and bare feet showed beneath her drawers. Her eyes looked dull, though firelight flickered in their dark depths. Her hair hung in a snarled, greasy mass that reached past where her hips must be.

"You must go away," she repeated weakly, choked, then doubled over again with racking coughs that seemed about to tear her delicate body apart.

"Dob Titwhistle is locked up, and Hera Coats lies snoring in the kitchen, past waking."

Maela's eyes widened. "Dob has seen thee? Oh, all is lost!" Her lips trembled. "Now he will know! He will discover my passage." She began to sob softly, gasping for breath.

"Nay, he saw not my face. Should I vanish, perchance he

will think 'twas a dream, or one of Hera's curses come to pass. Thy secret is yet safe."

Maela's eyes closed. Harry saw her sway. He leaped to catch her, and her weight was as nothing in his arms.

Maela awoke, but did not wish to open her eyes. Her dreams had been so wonderful that even their memory warmed her. Harry had stroked her face and arms as he spoke tender words of love and encouragement. Even now she caught the heady scent of him and inhaled deeply.

"It is well. You can breathe clearly now."

Maela's eyelids felt weighted, but she had to see if it were true. "Harry?" she whispered. His face came into focus. The room seemed filled with light. "Thou art truly here?" Her hand groped in his direction and felt his gentle squeeze.

"You do not remember?"

"I thought 'twas a dream."

"I know not how I will leave thee now that day has dawned, but I care not. Thy fever has broken, and thy cough is productive. I caused you to breathe an herbal mist while you slept. You have coughed up the congestion."

Maela thought this over. It sounded disgusting, but Harry did not look disgusted. "I dreamed. . ." she began. She lifted one arm into view. It was no longer grimy.

Reading her thoughts in her actions, Harry said soberly, "I rubbed thine arms and face with wet cloths, Maela, to bring down the fever. I knew not what else to do."

Maela thought her fever must have returned, for her face burned. Harry rose to prowl about the room. "I feared you would hate me, as you would have no man touch thee."

Far from feeling indignant, Maela wanted to beg for more. "Once you did tend my feet."

"Yea, but this time I did tend thee without thy consent."

"You have ever my full consent, Harry. I trust thee completely. This castle seems a brighter place, for I have seen thy face herein."

Harry brightened. "I hazarded thy wrath to make thee well and strong again. I cannot tell how I have missed thy presence this past se'ennight. The dogs miss thee, as well."

Maela smiled. "And I them. But. . .how did you come here? Grandmere. . .Dob. . .the curse—" Wonder creased her brow.

" 'Yea, though I walk through the valley of the shadow of death, I will fear no evil: for thou art with me,' " he quoted softly. "Thy grandmother slept, and God protected me from Dob. I saw none beside the twain."

"But how will you escape?"

"The secret tunnel?" Harry suggested. "I wish not to leave thee, but Dob will soon be discovered, and I fear thy grandmother will wish to ascertain thy continued presence. I have left bread, cheese, and apples here in this cloth at thy feet," he pointed. "I brought thee fresh water in a flask; it and two faggots for thy fire are hid in the garderobe. Now, I must require my cloak of thee."

Maela followed his glance and realized that she was wrapped snugly in his cloak. No wonder his scent had embraced her while she slept. Slowly she sat up and tried to unwrap its folds. Harry came to help her.

"There is a lever between two stones inside the fireplace in the great hall," Maela explained. "Reach up about thus far," she showed him the distance on her arm, "and pull it down. It is on the left behind a black stone. Harry," she paused, flushed, "I must use the garderobe."

Understanding her implied request, he helped her to her feet and into the side chamber, then left the room to allow her privacy. Maela remembered to wash her hands afterward this time, though the cold water added to the draft from the seat holes started her shivering again.

She crawled between her blankets and tried to soak up the warmth of the fire.

Harry knocked at her door. "Maela?" At her bidding, he reentered the room. She was nearly asleep already. Kneeling beside the pallet, he stroked her pale forehead lightly with his fingertips and watched her lips twitch into a smile. Through the night he had studied her face in detail while sponging away the grime. Delicate, feathery brows framed her eyes, and lush lashes brushed her cheeks as she slept. Her small ears were now rosy and clean; her pointed chin was determined but sweet. Someday she would be a prize that any man would be honored to claim. The unbidden thought brought him to his feet, frowning.

Quietly he closed the door of her chamber behind him. Slinking gingerly along the gallery, Harry peeked down the stairwell. All clear. Knife at the ready, he crept down the stairs and moved toward the great hall. Maela had told him it would be to his right, and sure enough, he stepped into the vast space of it a moment later. Somehow he had missed it during his explorations the night before. Far above was the gallery. He could just glimpse the top of the door to Maela's room. He felt less alone at sight of it.

The hall fireplace was immense. Maela must have been playing inside it when she discovered the lever, Harry decided. It was easily large enough for several children to play within. He searched for a black stone on the left side. There were several, but he soon found the right one. The lever pulled smoothly, and a narrow opening appeared in the paneled surround about two feet to the left of the fireplace. It had been invisible while closed. Harry couldn't help stopping to study it before entering.

Shouts reached his ears, and the sound of confusion. It was time to make haste. Slipping inside the tunnel, he slid the panel back into place and found himself in total darkness.

After a moment his heart began to beat again, and he remembered that Maela used this tunnel frequently. He was unlikely to become lost. Groping his way along the rock walls, bending nearly double beneath the low ceiling, he felt the tunnel slope downward beneath his feet. He took many hesitant steps, unsure of his footing. Suddenly the rock wall to his left ended, and Harry nearly fell into what turned out to be a shallow alcove. In it he felt wooden panels. A door? Maela hadn't mentioned that possibility. Was it the door he should take? Shaking his head in doubt, he kept walking ahead, hoping for a glimpse of daylight. It seemed he had been walking in darkness for an hour when at last a trickle of daylight dazzled his eyes. It came from above, and in its glow he saw jagged stone steps up the rock wall. Climbing with hands and feet, he pushed his head through bracken and popped up from the hole like a rabbit.

*Where am I?* He dared not wonder aloud. He was in a forest. A small hill rose behind him. Brambles caught at his cloak as he lifted himself from the hole. That explained Maela's perpetually scratched arms and legs.

It was a gray morning, just past dawn. An icy, misty rain was falling. A bird chirped hopefully from a nearby elm tree, and occasional scuffles in the underbrush indicated other small creatures. Harry crawled forward, searching for a place to stand erect. Brush scraped his hat from his head. When he paused to retrieve it, he glimpsed the castle keep just peeking above the hill at his back.

Of course! The hill was part of the ruined castle wall. The tunnel must have been intended as an escape route during siege.

There was no path through the wood, in spite of Maela's constant usage. The child must take care to leave no marks that might lead anyone to the tunnel entrance.

Skirting the castle road, Harry made his way cross-country through the forest. Coming out upon the main road about a mile from the cottage, he brushed dead leaves and gorse thorns from his hair, hat, and cloak, then struck out for home. He would scarcely have time to break his fast and care for the beasts before church began.

"Lord," he prayed aloud, "I thank Thee for Thy protection, guidance, and assurance of Thy complete power over any enemy, visible or invisible! And I thank Thee for Maela." His heart held far more, but he could not express it in words—or even in thought.

He broke into a jog, his breath forming frosty clouds.

Dob caused a minor stir when he was discovered and released. Old Balt, the nearly deaf and blind smithy who stayed in the castle stables, eventually heard him kicking at the storeroom door and released the latch. As soon as he was loose, Dob ran to the keep and shouted outside the kitchen door until Hera staggered to open it, bleary-eyed and prickly as nettles.

"An intruder! Did you fight off the intruder in the night?" he panted from the exertion of his short run.

Hera glared at him. "Thou art surely mad." Vitriolic epithets spewed from her tongue, but Dob ignored them.

"A man, a giant and powerful lord—nay, a wizard—wished to take the wench for ransom and demanded her location! He locked me in the storeroom, and Balt only now released me. Is she safe?"

Now somewhat concerned, Hera closed the door in his face and shuffled away. Dob waited on pins and needles for her return.

He did not wait long. "Thou dolt! Thou doddering idiot, to send me up those accursed stairs on a fool's errand! The child sleeps, and all is well within. You dreamed, or were in your cups."

Baffled, Dob took himself away to rehash the night's events. At length a plausible explanation dawned upon him.

" 'Twas the curse!" he told Balt firmly. "The rooks took that sorcerer! I heard them in the night, then a frightful scream; now, as you can see, they are gone. 'Twas the powers of darkness come upon us!" He crossed himself vigorously and pulled out his dried frog, a charm against witchcraft, to rub between his fingers.

When Balt eventually understood the gist of Dob's story, he also stared wide-eyed at the vacant battlements. Rooks had nested atop Castle Trent for many years. Now they were gone. There could be no other explanation.

## seven

*My son, preserve sound judgment and discernment,*
*do not let them out of your sight.*
Proverbs 3:21 (NIV)

Although Harry treasured his time with Maela, he also took pleasure in other activities. Sir David Marston threw feasts and dances nearly every holy day; the parish church was an excellent place to meet people, though not very good for worship; Trenton village held frequent concerts, pageants, meetings, and competitions. Harry participated in many of these. He and his dogs were well-known figures in the town.

Sports were more to his taste than the quieter pastimes. Harry romped with village boys and men, playing at football, ninepins, or battledore and shuttlecock. Fist fighting, bullbaiting, bearbaiting, and cockfighting seemed cruel sports to Harry, but he did appreciate an occasional dramatic play staged in Trenton's bearbaiting hall. He also participated in frequent archery matches and the required drill and weapon practice of the village militia. Along with every other man in Trenton between sixteen and sixty, Harry marched, lunged with a pike, clashed swords, loosed arrows, and fired an arquebus (matchlock gun).

One hot summer afternoon in 1566, more than a year after Harry's arrival at the manor, two female servants from Marston Hall brought drinks for the militia. While the men drilled, the women rested beneath a willow tree near the riverbank outside Trenton village and watched.

Waiting for his turn at the archery butt, Harry chatted with friends. Many of the men had already discarded their armor lest they faint of the sun's heat. Harry unbuckled his thick leather breastplate, dropped it on the grass, and heaved a sigh of relief. "I sympathize with the fate of a turtle," he jested.

"Oh, what a goodly man it is!" a freckled housemaid sighed as her dreamy eyes followed Harry's every move.

"Waste not thy time a-dreaming of the joiner, Lottie. He is overreligious and a doltish lout. He delivers abhorrent sermons to all and sundry. Surely you have not escaped unscathed from his double-edged tongue!" Dovie rolled her eyes in disgust and lay back on the grass.

Lottie looked doubtful, her eyes drinking in Harry as he drew his longbow, aimed, and shouted, "Fast!" His first shot just missed the bull's-eye.

"But he is strong and brave!" Lottie protested. "His skill at arms impresses even the men."

"Remove thine eyes from his fine limbs and goodly countenance, Lottie. They conceal a man whose character is beneath thy notice." Thus saying, Dovie allowed her own eyes to follow Harry's second shot. The arrow struck an outer ring of the target. "They say he despises women. No honest man will abide near him—therefore he lodges in the coppice cottage."

"I cannot believe this slander! Not only does Harry speak oft of God, he is exceedingly kind and good. I cannot believe that his nature is evil. Thy two charges lie at odds with one another!"

"Please thyself. I gave thee fair warning."

It was Lottie's first week at Marston Hall. She welcomed the break from household chores, for this had been her worst day yet.

Lottie had been assigned to pour drinks at dinner. After enduring sly winks and pinches from the field hands, which she had been unable to repel while holding a large pewter pitcher of ale, she had welcomed Harry's respectful manner.

"Have you any new milk?" he asked, refusing the double ale.

Opening her mouth to make a sharp reply, she met his gaze and stopped cold. " 'Twould pleasure me to fetch it for thee," she fluttered, and hurried to the dairy house.

His smile had rewarded her when she returned with the jug of milk, but to her dismay she had poured too fast, deluging his arm and lap. He had quickly leaped to his feet, brushing off his clothes. Not one word of blame, not one oath escaped his lips. He had refused her offer of help, claiming that the sun would soon dry him and that cold milk was good on a hot day—though he had never before applied it to his exterior. Lottie had gaped at him in silence, her blue eyes glazing over.

Palpitations of the heart seized her even now as she watched him hit the edge of the bull's-eye with his next shot. She clasped her hands at her breast, "Oh, well done, Harry!" Hearing her, he touched his helmet brim with a smile.

Another man heard Lottie's praise. When it came his turn to shoot, he picked up his bow, aimed quickly, and in rapid succession sent three bolts into the bull's-eye, dead center. He checked to make sure Lottie was watching, but her eyes followed Harry. The tall man frowned and retrieved his arrows with shoulders hunched.

"Impressive, Fleming," Harry remarked. "You do show us apprentices how it should be done."

Fleming acknowledged the compliment with a nod and watched as Harry joined the women under the tree. "Come hither, friend, and rest with us," Harry invited the older man, but Fleming pretended not to hear and drifted toward town.

"Please thyself." Harry pulled off his helmet and leather jerkin. Sweat drenched his body and trickled down his face; his hair was plastered to his head. His yearning gaze turned toward the river. "A swim would suit me well this day."

"Have a cup of ale?" Lottie offered, already dipping from the bucket. "We brought it for thy refreshment—and that of the other men."

"With pleasure." Harry drained the dipper in one long draught. He wiped his mustache with the back of one hand and smiled. "I thank thee, maiden. Thou art ever ready with a drink when I thirst, it seems."

"I hope so," Lottie simpered, finding it difficult to breathe. Only sixteen, Lottie had little experience with men, but she was eager to learn. Other sweaty weekend warriors gathered round, slaking their raging thirst and flirting with the women. They distracted Dovie, but Lottie saved her attention for Harry.

Dogs romped on the grass nearby—Laitha, Ragwort, a bloodhound, and two of Laitha's adolescent pups. One pup still belonged to Harry, the other to the town beadle. Laitha's pups had brought Harry a sizable profit. In a way he missed them, but the cottage was certainly more comfortable without them! The one pup he kept, a large, brindled male, was Maela's dog, Dudley.

Harry lay back at Lottie's feet, clasping his hands behind his head and gazing up into the willow's flowing branches. He took a deep breath, wondering how it would be if Maela could join him at these social activities. In his imagination she was clean, prettily clad, and enthralled by his athletic prowess. The admission brought a smile to his lips.

Lottie stared at him, not at all repulsed by the large damp patches on his stomach and beneath his arms, noting only how the coarse holland shirt clung to his brawny torso. Adolescent acne still marked his complexion, but Lottie focused upon his many fine features. Black hair curled upon his forearms and the strip of bare chest revealed by the open-necked shirt. Thick lashes and brows framed his pensive dark eyes. Shiny hair fell back from his broad forehead. One long leg was bent, the other stretched upon the grass.

Plain woolen trunk hose stopped at his knees. He had opted not to wear nether hose—probably due to the heat.

Lottie perused his recumbent figure once more from toe to head, and, upon reaching his face, was startled to find Harry's eyes upon her. "Do you think we are ready to fight the Irish should the queen require?" he asked.

Lottie immediately gushed, "Yea, of a truth, thou art prepared for anything!"

"The local militia fought in Ireland in recent years, so 'tis unlikely we will be called up soon."

George, a Marston Hall field hand, remarked, "I once heard

that Sir Hanover Trenton's grandfather received his knight-hood after brave fighting in Ireland under Henry the VII."

"Indeed?" Harry propped himself up on his elbows to listen. "And when passed the castle into Trenton hands?"

" 'Twas taken by the crown after a siege and awarded to the first Trenton. He was a good manager, unlike the present master. All know how Dob Titwhistle fills his own purse ere he sends the rent to Lord Trenton." George swallowed another dipper of ale.

Lottie felt left out. "Why does Lord Trenton not suspect?" She leaned forward to pick a burdock from Harry's hair, letting her fingers linger. His hair was damp with sweat, but soft, as she had anticipated. She began to brush leaves from the back of his shirt, but he sat up and moved out of her reach.

George chuckled. "He takes not the time to learn what monies he should receive. He has other properties, and likely other dishonest assessors. The castle itself falls to ruin, and he cares nothing for it. His mind is taken up with Good Queen Bess and international affairs."

"Does he court the queen? I hear she has countless suitors," Lottie inquired. Romance of any kind fascinated her.

"He is a married man, else he would likely top the list of hopefuls. That Austrian archbishop has given up hope of her. The Frog king, though half her age, has hopes—or perhaps they're his mother's hopes. The Earl of Leicester holds our queen's heart, 'tis rumored, but she should ne'er marry him."

"Why not?"

"His wife died in suspicious circumstances. It can never be proven, but should he marry the queen, many would say he murdered his first wife to make himself free. He is beneath Her Majesty in birth, rank, and all else, yet she favors him. His fine figure and comely face hold her fancy, though she loves him not enough to make him king. Nevertheless, Parliament pressures her to marry and provide an heir to the throne."

"I pity her," Harry remarked.

"You pity Her Most Royal Highness, the queen of England and Wales?" George scoffed. "I would take her place."

"I would not. She fears to marry, I think, lest she lose her power and the love of her husband. Mind her sister's fate. Queen Mary's marriage brought heartbreak and disaster—and no heir."

" 'Tis noised," Dovie jumped into the discussion, "that the Scot queen's husband, Lord Darnley, has murdered her secretary, David Rizzio."

"Of a truth?" Lottie's eyes were enormous. "For what cause?"

"Jealousy, if talk be true. The queen did love the man."

Harry pressed his point. "Her cousin's unhappy marriage cannot encourage Queen Elizabeth to seek a husband."

"Yet the Scot queen has at least provided an heir to the throne," George observed.

None of them dared voice the thought aloud, but all knew that Mary, Queen of Scots, was a threat to Elizabeth's sovereignty. Although the Protestant government of Scotland was continually at odds with their Catholic queen, many in England considered Mary Stuart their rightful queen. Elizabeth's position as legitimate heir was in serious question. Her parents' marriage had been declared invalid so that Henry VIII could marry again. Was she the rightful queen? It was a ticklish situation, at best.

❧

"Harry, the purpose of this is unclear to me." Maela obediently stirred the kettle of hot fat while Harry poured in the lye, but a frown wrinkled her brow. " 'Twould surely profit me more to pursue my studies in Latin this day. What is the purpose of making soap? Can you not take some in trade if it is needed?"

Harry glanced up long enough to appreciate her little pout. "The soap will be of use to us."

"Of use to us, indeed. You wish to smell pretty for that housemaid. I have beheld her with thee at militia drill."

This arrested Harry's attention. "You have witnessed the practice sessions?"

"It pleases me to behold thee. But it pleases me not to see

that. . .that wench behold thee!"

Harry chuckled. "You speak in riddles. Do I hear the rantings of a jealous woman?"

Maela's face was already as flushed as it could be while she worked over the boiling soap, but Harry saw her bite her lip and cringe from his words. "Maela, I do but jest. Once I beheld the exquisite visage of a maiden—but, alas, this day her beauty is veiled from my sight. I would see her face once more, and this soap may aid me toward that end."

Maela looked narrowly at him, suspecting a hidden meaning. "Do I know this maiden?"

"You have heard me mention her name—Maela, the soap thickens." Harry changed the subject, hoping to distract her.

Since Maela's illness he had not seen her hair; she kept it bundled beneath a cap. He wondered how long it had been since she combed it out, but never dared ask. Most people were undismayed by fetid body odors, for they all stank alike, but Harry came from a family that valued biblical cleanliness.

Harry not only wanted Maela clean for his own sake; he also worried about her health. Maela was seldom close enough for her body odor to bother him, but he worried about parasites. Some people took lice and fleas for granted; Harry was not among them.

Maela was not to be distracted. "It is that Lottie. She haunts thee like a spirit, I trow, and you enjoy her worship."

"Cease this foolish babble. Lottie is a silly child, no more. Have you spied upon me at the manor as well, wench?"

Maela glared at him. "Upon occasion. Seldom have I seen thee without that freckled wench in tow. If she is a child, what am I?"

"A younger child. Nay, in truth, she is thine inferior in understanding, Maela, though superior in years. Envy her not. Thy jealousy is wasted upon her."

"Thou art too kind and gentle—her affection thrives on thy kindness."

The soap thickened into sludge. Harry was not sure what to

do next, for in spite of his boasts to Maela, he had never made soap before. He began to ladle it into pots and pails while Maela watched. "Her interest thrives on air. I give her no encouragement," he grumbled. Lottie's hero worship had begun to annoy him long before Maela pointed it out. "To be sure, she makes no indecent proposals, unlike others. She is a chaste and worthy maiden."

Wondering about this comment, Maela asked, "What indecent proposal might she make?"

"Why. . .uh. . .she. . ." Harry dithered, then busied himself, awkwardly pouring the soap. It slopped over the top of one pail, then another. He was creating a slimy mess in the yard of his cottage. Evidently, he had not given the location of his soap-making project enough forethought.

Maela dipped a finger into the cooled product and lifted it to her nose. "Will you place this foul stuff upon thy body?"

"I shall add lavender scent to it," Harry assured her.

"When?"

"Now." He sprinkled a liberal amount of dried lavender blossoms into each container and bade her stir it in. Maela obeyed, grimacing at the result.

"Now it stinks and has flowers in it. What will you do with this. . .mess?"

"Wash my raiment and my body with it," he asserted bravely, though a closer examination gave him pause.

"Better thou than me!"

# eight

*Oh Lord, thou preservest man and beast.*
Psalm 36:6

One September morning, Harry awoke to find that a wild creature had broken into his chicken coop. Feathers littered the yard; Sage and Rosemary were gone. Only poor Parsley perched atop her ravaged house, squawking distractedly, and would not allow Harry to touch her. The dogs had failed to sound an alarm at the crucial time. Ragwort snuffled and snarled around the coop, and made short dashes into the forest, barking a challenge, but the damage was already done.

Harry left work early that day and started repairing and strengthening the coop. It would not be difficult to replace the hens; he was more concerned about Maela's reaction, for she was deeply attached to every one of his animals. Selling the buck kids had nearly broken her tender heart, though Harry had assiduously avoided mentioning their probable fate.

Harry glanced over his shoulder and was surprised to find Maela standing behind him. "Good morrow, child. A sorry day is this." After tapping a peg into place, he tried to stand up and bashed his head on the low doorway of the coop. "Ahh," he grimaced, rubbing the sore spot.

Maela stared at him, her face pinched and sober. He squinted at her out of one eye. "A stoat or weasel carried off two hens, some creature small and strong. Parsley alone is with us still."

The girl nodded, her lips pressed together.

Harry noticed a lack. "Where is Pegasus?" he asked, glancing around the yard. "Did you walk this day?"

Maela turned away, her slender shoulders quaking, and lowered her face into her hands.

In two steps Harry stood before her. "Dead? Ill? What has become of him?" he demanded.

"I know not; only that his pasture is empty," she gasped. "I believe Dob has taken him and the cart horses to market." She burst into tears, something he had never before seen her do.

Harry swallowed hard. He patted her shoulder awkwardly, uncertain how to react to her tears. Spinning options through his mind, he finally stated, "Today is market day in Hently. I shall attempt to find thy horse. Care for the others in mine absence."

He took more than the price of a pony from his hidden store of coins and stuffed it into the hanging pocket tied to his belt. Tossing his cloak over one shoulder, he bade Maela pray for success and struck the road toward Hently, a market town north of Trenton.

Hours later he believed himself on the right trail. One merchant recalled seeing a burly stranger with a chestnut pony and two cart horses for sale, and he pointed Harry to another merchant who had talked to the seller. This merchant directed Harry to a farm some five miles to the southwest, where he believed the pony's buyer lived. It was a long walk for an uncertain outcome, but Harry was willing to try.

To his surprise, the directions led him, by a circuitous route, to a farm near the outskirts of Marston Hall property. The bleak outline of Castle Trent keep was visible above the treetops as Harry approached the farmhouse.

A slender, pleasant-faced yeoman emerged from the barn. "God give you good day," he greeted respectfully. Harry had seen the man before, but did not know his name.

"And you," Harry replied, bowing in return, then extended his hand. "Harold Jameson, joiner at Marston Hall."

"Well met, Jameson. I know you by reputation and have seen you at church. I am called Jonas Fleming. May I give you aid?" Fleming had a firm handshake.

"I trust that you may. I seek a chestnut gelding, nigh eleven hands, no markings, sold this day at market. A merchant told me I might find it here."

"Verily, my son purchased such a horse this day. His mother did wish for a pony to drive. Is it stolen?" The farmer's face was troubled.

"Nay, but I know the horse well, and would have purchased it had I known 'twould go to market. 'Tis a child's pet and well loved."

"Ah, indeed." The yeoman scrutinized Harry's youthful face, wondering about this unknown child. " 'Twas Master Dob of Castle Trent that sold it, you know."

Harry nodded. "But the pony belonged to Lord Trenton's daughter, and she consented not to part with it." Something prompted him to trust Fleming with Ishmaela's secret. "I am her tutor and friend, unbeknownst to Dob Titwhistle or Mistress Hera. The child is a believer, and greatly in need of friends, Master Fleming."

The farmer's bearded cheeks creased in a wide smile. "I thought you had the look of the redeemed. Might you take an interest in our Bible study meetings? Many church members meet independently to search the Scriptures each week."

Before Harry could answer, a younger man emerged from the barn, laid eyes on Harry, and stopped short. "Jameson?"

"Fleming! This is thine abode?"

"Indeed."

"Thou art acquainted?" Master Fleming observed with pleasure.

"Militia," Lane explained. "Jameson excels at broadsword."

"And thou art expert with the longbow." Harry grinned. Despite his best efforts to be friendly, he had never exchanged more than two or three sentences with Fleming, for the man was painfully shy.

Before long Harry was seated at the farmhouse's rough board, sharing his life story over a tankard of milk and a loaf of bread. Lane Fleming sat opposite. He was a clean-shaven man in his late twenties, as long and lean as his mother was short and wide.

Mistress Rachel Fleming was fascinated by the story of Ishmaela Andromeda Trenton, filling in a few gaps for Harry from her own memory. "I knew Hera Coats many years ago, and her daughter Artemis as well. Old Reuben Coats was a fine tailor and a decent man, worthy of a better wife. Hera was a comely woman, but Artemis's beauty surpassed her mother's by far. Like the goddess of her name she was, white of skin, formed to perfection, with hair of spun gold. After Reuben's untimely death, Hera saw opportunity in the lass and put her in Sir Hanover's way. Being the carnal man he is, his lordship was overcome by desire and made Artemis his mistress."

Harry was accustomed to crude speech from kitchen maids and field hands, but blunt speech from this wholesome farmwife embarrassed him. He wished she would not speak of sin with such apparent relish. He glanced at Lane, but the other man did not bat an eye. Of course, he must be used to his mother's active tongue.

"Sir Hanover was a well-favored man with flashing dark eyes. Artemis was flattered by his attentions and believed herself in love. She was soon found to be with child. Overjoyed at the prospect of an heir, Sir Hanover showered her with gifts and gave her proud standing in the community. Most knew of his previous marriage, however, and secretly despised Artemis for throwing her virtue away with both hands."

Mistress Rachel finally noticed Harry's discomfiture. "I do abash thee, lad? Art thou married thyself?"

He gave a quick shake of his head. "Nay."

Her rosy cheeks crinkled when she smiled. "Not for lack of takers, I'll wager." She patted Harry's shoulder as she rose to refill his tankard. "Lane, here, is besieged by local females, and thou, too, art a fine figure of a man, Harry the joiner. More milk?"

"Nay, but I thank thee." He covered the tankard with one hand. Wishing to resume the former subject, he inquired, "Have you seen the child, Ishmaela?"

"Nay, but Jonas would have it that you know the maid."

"That I do, and well. It was a year ago last May that I met her first. The pony was hers, though how she manages to ride it daily without Dob's notice is a puzzle."

"Dob notices little beyond his nose," Lane observed through a mouthful of bread. "The man cares solely for his own comfort. However, he is deadly with the longbow." For a moment he lifted vivid blue eyes to meet Harry's gaze. It wasn't exactly a smile, but an amiable expression flashed across his craggy features.

Harry's brows lifted. "I shall keep that in mind."

Rachel calculated in her head. "The maid is nigh unto fifteen years of age. Do you think to wed her, Harry?"

Hot blood flooded Harry's face. He couldn't manage to close his mouth for a moment. "She. . .she is but a child, mistress."

"Fie! Do you love the maid?" It was more of a statement than a question.

"Yea, verily, she is dear to me." Strange emotions rippled beneath his conscious thoughts. Rachel's smug smile irked him.

"I would see this child of Artemis and Sir Hanover, this Ishmaela Andromeda." She chuckled at the mental image such a name invoked. "Will you bring her to us?"

Harry hedged, "Perhaps." The last thing he needed was a nosy old woman to plant suspicions and ideas in Maela's innocent head!

"I am sorry to lose the new pony, but of a certain he must be returned. The child has little else to call her own. Lane shall find me another." Rachel beamed at her son, who did not respond. Harry deduced that Lane simply tuned out much of his mother's prattle, though he did speak to her with respect.

In the end, Jonas and Lane accepted a reasonable price for Pegasus and agreed to keep him in their back pasture, where Ishmaela should be able to collect him easily for her daily rides. The Flemings were husbandmen, but they also raised fine Suffolk cart horses. Pegasus would never want for company, though he would be dwarfed by his companions.

Walking home late that night, Harry whistled cheerfully. A more generous answer to his prayers for help could not have been imagined. Maela's pony was presently tearing mouthfuls of grass from a rich pasture in an ideal location—with Dob none the wiser. Harry also carried a burlap sack full of two clucking pullets; a certain softhearted farmwife couldn't bear to think of a child losing her pony and two pet hens all in one day.

As an extra bonus, Harry had received a personal invitation to attend Bible study services. During his sojourn at the manor he had attended the village church as the law required, making do with the small amount of spiritual sustenance he gleaned from the vicar's dry sermons. Now he had opportunity to worship with other committed believers. He liked the Flemings, in spite of, or perhaps partially because of, Rachel's nosy, motherly ways. Jonas was a pleasant man, and Lane seemed to be an interesting personality.

Harry's cottage was quiet, though smoke trickled from the chimney. After depositing the pullets in the repaired coop, he opened the cottage door quietly. Maela lay curled up on the hearth before the flaring coals with Laitha as a pillow, Ragwort snuggled against the small of her back, Dudley in the curve of her legs, and Parsley peacefully roosting in the crook of her arm.

Dudley's tail whacked the floor, and he lifted his head in greeting. Harry squatted at Maela's feet, searching her face in the dim light. His tender smile faded into a frown. What would become of the two of them? This idyllic existence could not continue forever.

"Ishmaela," he called softly. "Ishmaela, I have come home." A pang shot through his heart. This was his home, but only because she was here. "Maela, wake up." He tickled her cheek.

Ragwort stretched and hopped into Harry's lap. Laitha quivered but did not rise. Parsley gave a protesting gargle when Maela rolled to her back and sat up, rubbing her eyes with the back of one hand. The girl blinked; then her eyes grew wide as memory returned. "Harry! Did you find him?"

"Yea, of a truth I found thy pony and redeemed him for thee."

"Oh, Harry!" She burst into tears for the second time that day and flung both arms about his neck. Harry sat down with a thump, then fell flat on his back with his knees in the air. Maela fell upon him; Ragwort narrowly escaped being crushed by her. He yipped in protest and tugged at Harry's sleeve. Laitha sat up and whimpered. Dudley barked. The chicken fluttered across the room, clucking in fright.

Harry laughed helplessly. "Such a to-do! Why do you weep, child? I tell you the pony is found, and even now he grazes in rich pasture. You shall have him on the morrow; I'll take you to him." Harry patted her back uncertainly, then sighed and hugged her. She was heavier than he remembered. She was warm in his arms—warm, trembling, and alive. Her head rested in the hollow of his shoulder, her cheek pressed to his chest.

Suddenly Maela pulled away, her tear-streaked face averted. "I must go home," she mumbled. "I thank thee, Harry."

Before he could say a word, she had dashed out the door and vanished into the night.

# nine

*Therefore I say unto you, what things soever ye desire,*
*when ye pray, believe that ye receive them,*
*and ye shall have them.*
Mark 11:24

Maela's new pullets, two red hens with shining feathers, settled quickly into the repaired chicken coop and thrived under
her tender care. Within months, they were each producing at
least one egg a day. Maela named them Thyme and Pepper.

Harry saw the Flemings at Bible study and at church each
week, but, as yet, he did not feel comfortable bringing Maela.
One evening, Rachel cornered him. "Harry, lad, when will
you bring the lass to meeting? She needs fellowship with
other maids; and I perish to meet her."

"I. . .I am uncertain," Harry stuttered lamely. "She has little
experience in society. Her raiment is tattered, and. . .I fear
that once her existence is widely known, 'twill make her life
difficult."

"I am certain that the brethren would be prudent, Harry. We
would show only kindness and acceptance to the child. Not
one of us lacks sorrow and sin in our past lives. We have no
cause to judge a child for the sins of her parents."

Harry remained unconvinced.

It was spring again, a chilly spring that year of 1567. The
weather dampened many spirits; yet in at least one young
girl's heart, thoughts of love predominated. Lottie's devotion
could not be quenched, and Harry's steadfast rejection of her
overtures brought about unforeseen results.

One afternoon when Harry arrived home, Maela exploded
from the cottage door in a whirlwind of excitement. He

laughed aloud at her capers. "Child, I know few other maidens who come aflutter over a fishing venture. To be more accurate, I know of none beside thee!"

"Then other maidens lack wisdom and interest," she retorted, skipping about like a rabbit.

"I'll not argue that point," he admitted. "Now hark; I shall return quickly."

Harry entered the shed and emerged with fishing poles and a wicker creel. The jolly pair hiked down the river path with the dogs leaping at their heels. Once Laitha turned back and growled softly, but they took no notice of her. Maela boasted that she would catch the largest fish. Harry assured her that she was mistaken.

At last the pair settled upon the riverbank. "I do enjoy the spring. Snow is gone; the air is cool and delicious—like wine should taste, but doesn't. Have you ever tasted wine, Harry? A dire disappointment it was to me. From here we can see for many miles. The land is like a plowed field—it undulates. Is the sea like that, Harry? Ever have I wished to look upon the sea. Is it like the river, but much more broad? The river is high this day, Harry. The rains have swollen it. I like not how the brown water swirls about these tree trunks. Our customary fishing spot is under water."

Harry managed to slip in a reply. "Indeed, the river is high. The current runs strong, though not fast. We shall remain in this shallow place and cast out into the deep. Bait thy hook, Maela, and lower thy voice. I care not to have thee frighten the fish."

"The water roars far louder than I, Harry."

"But not so rapidly."

Maela wrinkled her nose at him, but obediently baited her hook and cast her line. It was a windy afternoon. The sinking sun occasionally peeked between rushing gray clouds, casting its golden light upon gently rolling terrain. Trees wore a pale green glaze of newly budding leaves, while delicate wildflowers peeked through soggy mulch.

Maela's line went taut. She threw off her cloak and pulled with all her strength. The lissome rod bent nearly double.

Harry propped up his rod, stood behind her, and together they gave a great jerk. A flopping fish flew over their heads and landed in a wild rose bramble. Maela laughed at the sight of Harry wading into the prickly bushes to retrieve her fish.

"You do laugh like a fool this day, Maela!" Harry chided her. "Calm thyself, child. The county shall be up in arms to defend against this lunatic in our midst!"

She tried to gain control, but still giggled occasionally. Harry relented and smiled at her. She did have a cute giggle, and once in a while he spotted a shallow dimple in her cheek when she grinned at him. It was good to hear the once sober child laugh freely.

She admired her gleaming trout as it lay, twitching feebly, in the creel. "It shall give us a sumptuous feast this night."

Then Harry's rod jerked. "What ho!" he shouted in delight. It was a powerful fish. Harry slipped upon the wet grass and accidentally sloshed into the shallows, still fighting that fish. His boots filled with water. Maela followed him without considering how cold the water must be. She gave a yelp at its icy bite, but, undeterred, reached for the line, trying to grasp the fish before it could pull free. Dudley stood behind her on the bank, barking in excitement.

"Go to, child! I can do this," Harry protested. "Have a care; the bottom drops off steeply just beyond thee there." He grasped the line and hauled in his fish, a magnificent tench that still fought to be free as it dangled from his hand. "Now, who has caught the largest fish this day, eh?"

He looked at Maela, but her startled attention was focused behind him.

Ragwort barked hysterically—a piercing scream rent the air—something came crashing down the bank. Dudley dodged, tail between his legs.

Harry pivoted, but his boots would not move. He barely had time to see a body rushing toward him before it barreled past, collided with the tench dangling from his hand, and hit Maela with an ugly thud and a splash. Harry sat down in the water, losing his boots entirely.

He quickly scrambled up, shouting at the cold shock. The fish was gone. His pole was gone. Rising from the water beside him was Lottie, drenched and wailing. Maela was. . .

"Maela?"

Harry spun about, and could only watch in shock as Maela surfaced several yards away, sputtering, arms flailing. Her eyes entreated Harry, but her open mouth only took in water. Weighted by her sodden skirts and boots, she was again pulled helplessly under, caught by the relentless current, and swept away.

Harry left his boots in the mud and sprinted barefoot along the bank, crashing through shrubs and saplings as he kept his eyes upon Maela's bobbing figure. At last he caught up and passed her, then launched himself into the river in a wild dive. He thought he had missed her, but then his hand connected with fabric. He grabbed hold and pushed for the shore, pulling her along with him. At this point the river was not deep. Harry found his footing, lifted Maela's limp body into his arms, and sloshed heavily ashore.

Lottie trudged along the bank, wringing the edges of her sodden kirtle. "Is she dead?" Lottie gasped. "Who is she?"

Harry had no breath to spare for explanations. He pressed his ear to Maela's chest and thought he heard a faint heartbeat, though he could not be certain. Placing her face down, he turned her head to the side and began to push rhythmically on her back. Her mouth hung open; her eyes were closed. She was white and cold.

"Oh, God, please," Harry choked, gasping for his own breath. Still he pushed, but there was no response. Rolling her suddenly to her back, he pressed upon her chest and stomach, striving to push air into her body. He thought he saw movement in her face, but then she was still.

He turned her face down again, almost fell upon her in his desperation, crushing her beneath him and pressing, rolling. Tears poured from his eyes, but he was unaware. "God, grant me this boon! Oh, God, I love her so! Spare Maela, God, I beg of Thee!"

Lottie watched with wide, unblinking eyes. Ragwort and Dudley stood beside her, ears pricked, expressions worried. Earlier Laitha had been wandering in the woods, but now she appeared, looking concerned, though she could neither see nor understand the crisis at hand.

Then Maela choked. Water trickled from her mouth, her body convulsed, and a gush of water poured forth. She coughed, retched, vomited, and writhed upon the ground.

Harry was ecstatic. "I thank Thee, O my God! Thy goodness is everlasting!" Rocking back on his heels as he squatted beside Maela, he lifted his hands to the skies and wept now for joy.

"Harry?" Maela croaked. "I'm so cold!" Her teeth chattered audibly. Her face was ashen.

Harry scooped her into his arms and marched back to their fishing spot. He wrapped her in her dry cloak, donned his own cloak, picked up the fishing rod and the creel with Maela's fish and handed them to Lottie. "Carry these."

Lottie grimaced, but dared not quibble.

Harry swung Maela back into his arms. Her cap was gone, lost in the river. One of her boots was missing. Her little bare foot swung high in the air as Harry shifted her weight more evenly. Maela was too weak to protest, though her white fingers grasped at his cloak.

Harry did not intend to be rough, but his tangled emotions preoccupied him. Gratitude for Maela's recovery, fear that she would become ill, anger with Lottie, embarrassment at the intensity of feeling he had displayed, worry about the future, exhaustion. . .

He determined to take Maela to the Flemings. Rachel would know how to care for her. She needed a woman's care; Harry was out of his depth.

Not until they were walking along the road did Lottie dare try to explain her presence, "I followed after thee, but then a wolf did howl in mine ear and I ran to thee, but the bank was steep and I could not stop. I did not intend to knock this. . . person into the river."

"Yonder is thy wolf," Harry nodded at the terrier trotting briskly ahead of them. "His bark is greater than his stature. You did deserve thy ducking, spy. Almost I hope you fall ill of a fever." His voice sounded flat.

"The dog sounded large; indeed, it did. And I am most dreadfully cold!" Lottie shivered daintily. She wore no cloak, and her damp kirtle kept wrapping about her legs, making it difficult to walk. She hitched it up into her girdle, leaving only her smock to conceal her legs. Light brown curls escaped her cap to bounce upon her shoulders. "Who is this maid, Harry? I know her not. Has she no comb? Never have I seen such filthy hair."

Harry could hardly blame her for noticing. Maela's long hair swung over his arm in a heavy, dripping, matted clump. It was disgusting, but Lottie's comments were cruel. He felt Maela flinch.

"Have done!" he growled. He had frequently noticed that Lottie was no sweet-smelling rose herself, but he did not say so. She was a top-heavy, ruddy wench. Harry was not attracted by her obvious charms.

It was nearly dark, and the wind was rising. It whipped through Harry's cloak, slapping it around his boot tops. If he was this cold, how must Maela feel? He walked faster. Lottie puffed along, trotting at times to keep up.

"Where are we going?" she demanded. "This is not the way to Marston Hall."

"We go to the Fleming freehold. I would have Mistress Fleming care for Maela's needs."

Maela stiffened. Harry could not read her expression, but he felt tension in her every limb.

"Wherefore did you follow me, Lottie?" Harry would have the truth of the matter.

"I. . .I came to discern if Dovie told the truth about thee. In truth, you speak often with women, and your manner is all gallantry—but all agree that no maiden in the county have you touched. It is unnatural for a man that is not a priest! There is talk that thou art. . ." Lottie faltered. Her teeth began to chatter.

Harry stopped abruptly and turned. He looked as though he

had been punched in the stomach. "Is this what is said concerning me? That I am . . . depraved? Unnatural?"

Lottie nodded, wiping her nose on her damp apron. "Yet not I, Harry! I know thou art a true man!" Her blue eyes glimmered in the light of a pale half moon.

Maela emitted a sound not unlike a growl.

Lottie glanced her way. "Is this wench thy lover?"

Harry's voice was dry. "She is but a child. I have no lover; but had I a lover, 'twould most certainly be my lawfully wedded wife!"

"I would marry thee, Harry," Lottie offered hopefully. "I would be a good wife to thee."

With surprising strength, Maela began to struggle. Harry lost his grip, and her feet fell to the road. She scrambled up and tried to run, but he grasped her cloak, pulled her back, and held her, squirming and grunting, against his chest. Not this time would Maela run off to the castle!

"Ishmaela, you did but narrowly escape death this day," he reminded firmly.

"Release me!" she ordered. Were tears clogging her voice?

"Nay, I will not." Harry's voice gave no quarter.

"I would return to the castle." Her voice was stony.

"I take thee to the house of friends who will care for thee. Give them opportunity to show thee love, Maela. They are brethren in Christ and of thy grandmother's age."

Her little figure went limp. She nodded in surrender.

Harry scooped her up and returned to Lottie's side.

Lottie had not lost her train of thought. "Do you not think I would make thee a good wife? I can cook and clean, and I would give thee many children."

"I need no wife at present," Harry growled, panting in near exhaustion. Much though he loved her, Maela was a dead weight in his aching arms. Her teeth chattered and she shivered convulsively.

The Fleming farmhouse reached out to them in welcome. Its windows were warmly lighted. Smoke drifted from the flint chimney.

"Rachel?" Harry called out between puffs. His great chest heaved; his heart pounded.

The door opened before they reached it. "Harry the joiner? Wherefore do you stroll about at this hour—"

She broke off abruptly. "Who is that with thee? What are you holding?"

"These are Lottie Putnam—from the manor—and Ishmaela Trenton—who is nigh drowned and freezing. I bring them to thee for aid!" he explained between pants.

With many exclamations and much clucking, Rachel ushered them inside and bade them sit before the crackling fire. Harry hugged Maela closer, but she resisted his embrace and would not look at him.

Lottie held her hand out to the fire's warmth and hitched up her skirts to warm her legs. "I knew not how cold a body can be," she tried to joke.

"Lane!" Rachel called out the door. "Tell Longwell to bring the washtub inside." She bustled about, giving orders to her hapless maidservant. "You need hot baths, all. The maidens first, of a certain."

Rachel ordered them all to strip, so Harry went into the sitting room for privacy. It was cold, for no fire burned upon its hearth. He handed his clothing through the door. "I remain here while the maidens do bathe," he insisted; though Rachel argued that he would surely freeze. He'd been right to come here; Rachel had things well in hand.

The blanket Rachel had given him itched terribly, but at least it was dry. He bundled into it, lay down upon the wooden settle, and fell asleep.

Lane entered the kitchen. His curious gaze swept the room, taking in the two blanket-shrouded females beside the fire. Rachel hastened to explain and introduced the young women to him. Maela only nodded, too tired to speak. Lane took one look at Lottie and started visibly. She met his eyes and smiled in her friendly way.

"Good even, Master Lane Fleming."

His blue eyes glowed. "Charlotte Putnam. We meet at last.

God is very good."

At this interesting point, Rachel chased him from the room. "The maidens must bathe. Out with thee!"

"A quiet man. He is. . .unwed?" Lottie asked with interest. She tested the water.

While hanging Harry's clothing to dry upon a trivet and a chair, Rachel examined the plump girl critically, then seemed to approve her. "Verily, Lane is our only living son. He is, as yet, unwed."

Lottie climbed into the tub and settled herself with a sigh. "This is a fine house, and your son is a goodly man. I have heard your name noised in town."

Rachel followed her thoughts with no trouble. Lane stood to inherit the family farm—an enticing prospect to many a single female. "And thy family is located where?" she asked the girl.

"Beyond Hently. My father is husbandman on the land of Sir Giles Thorpe."

Bending over Maela, Rachel pulled aside her blanket. "Ah, the poor maid. She sleeps. She is the picture of her mother, though dirty and unkempt. I shall soon make a thing of beauty from this rough fabric." Turning, she asked, "Do you need soap, Lottie Putnam?"

"If you please."

❧

"Harry, waken!" Rachel insisted, shaking his shoulder. "Thy bath water awaits."

Harry jumped and sat up, rescuing his blanket just in time. His brain scrambled to recall why he was here.

He blinked groggily at Rachel. "Maela?"

"She sleeps. Lane has escorted thine other maiden to the manor, for she must not neglect her work. A buxom lass, that one, and fair. Do you admire her?"

Harry smiled fleetingly. "Lane may have her with my blessing. Maela is not ill?" He returned to his major concern.

"Not as yet. A long soak in hot water did she require ere her skin warmed to the touch. I did soap her hair three times ere the rinse water ran clear. It would not comb, so I cut a length of it from her. Thou art welcome to stay the night, Harry, thou and thy dogs. I'll prepare a pallet for thee nigh the fire."

Rachel and Jonas retired to their bedchamber while Harry bathed. Maela was already settled in the loft over the kitchen. Harry's dogs snored contentedly beside the fire.

He bent to rinse his hair with the pitcher. Soapy water cascaded over his face and dripped back into the tub. His knees jutted nearly under his chin, but at least the water was hot and the soap didn't have wilted little flowers in it.

# ten

*Shout for joy, O heavens; rejoice, O earth; burst into song, O mountains! For the Lord comforts his people and will have compassion on his afflicted ones.*
Isaiah 49:13 (NIV)

Maela felt like a new girl. She pulled her hair over her shoulder and studied its color and texture. Spreading her fingers upon her kirtle, she smoothed it over her hips. Standing in the doorway to soak up a brief patch of early spring sunshine, she twisted her hips back and forth to make the borrowed kirtle swirl about her legs.

She seemed to have taken no permanent harm from her near drowning, and though her chest ached if she breathed too deeply, the pain grew less with each passing hour. Her memories of the day before were fuzzy and troubling.

But for now, she was happy. Her borrowed smock was clean and white. The blue linen kirtle had lain in Rachel's wooden chest since the death of her daughter seventeen years ago; now it hugged Maela's slim waist and swirled about her legs in a satisfying way. It smelled strongly of lavender.

Rachel smiled as she watched the girl preen. An amazing transformation, she congratulated herself. Having seen the matted, greasy mop that once topped the girl's head, Rachel would never have guessed that her hair would be of such remarkable color and texture. Dark red without a hint of curl, it flowed smoothly over the girl's shoulders, gleaming like heavy silk.

"Mistress Rachel," Maela spoke quietly, looking at Rachel with almost reverent eyes. "Did you know my mother?"

Rachel stopped kneading the bread dough for an instant,

then resumed her work. "Yea, I did know her better than some. She was of an age with our youngest daughter, Agnes, whose kirtle you wear with such pleasure."

Maela nodded, having already heard Agnes's sad story. Of the Flemings' seven children, only Lane had reached adulthood. A small family cemetery lay behind the Fleming barn. "And Agnes did know my mother?"

"Many's the time I did hear the twain chatter like starlings as they drew water and washed clothing together. Thy mother was surpassing fair, yet not so wise as Agnes, for she did like men overmuch. Hera, her mother, did push the maid to be forward, to her great cost." Rachel sighed.

Maela's eyes were sad. "I was that cost?"

Rachel started. "May God forbid that you should think such foolishness, child! You were your mother's joy and comfort amid sorrow. I doubt not she did love you greatly, and desired you to know the truths that she came to know too late. Artemis was lovely in her heart, as you well know. 'Twas her bane and her blessing to be among the fairest of women and to provoke the lust of Sir Hanover Trenton."

"Beauty, therefore, is a bane? But I so desire to be beautiful to please. . .to. . .to. . ." Maela's cheeks flushed crimson.

"Nay, 'tis not wicked in thee to desire to please thy man, and he shall be well pleased in thee, child. Like a flower thou art, in appearance and in scent. These things do please a man."

"Lottie is. . .is round where I am. . .not. He does admire her, I know. I hate her." Maela's dark eyes smoldered.

Rachel said nothing, but a little smile tugged at her lips. She shaped the dough into round loaves and left them to rise.

"It is wicked to hate," Maela reminded her as though prompting a reprimand.

"I think thy sin is envy, not hatred. I did not answer thee promptly because thy words brought back memories of thy mother saying much the same words—not to me, but to Agnes while in my hearing. Thy mother was a slender child until later than most, but when she did bloom into womanhood, the transformation was complete. You do waste thine envy upon a poor maid." She chuckled. "You will cause weeping and gnashing of teeth, child. The maidens shall cast one look at thee and despair!"

"But why, Rachel? I understand so little. What is it that maidens do desire of men? What is it that makes my breath come short when Harry smiles at me? Why does my flesh burn where'er his hand touches me? I long to touch him, to hold him, yet almost I fear to be near him lest he behold these longings in mine eyes. He cares for me yet as a child, and such kindness is to me as bitter gall! I cannot comprehend this change in me, and I know not what to do! Surely, I cannot speak of this to Harry; yet I know none else in the world—save thee."

"Oh, thou innocent child, bereft of thy mother! Surely I shall counsel thee in any manner you desire. Come and sit beside me, and we shall speak privately of many things."

Rachel was true to her word and generous with her time. While the bread rose, great mysteries of womanhood that had puzzled Maela for months were at last resolved to her complete satisfaction.

The girl quietly pondered the information she had been given, while Rachel braided her hair. Color came and went in Maela's smooth cheeks, and smiles flitted across her lips. "Shall Harry come here this night?" she asked. "I wish to speak with him. Yet, verily, I must return to the castle, for I shall be missed. I wish not to cause thee trouble."

"Thou art no trouble, child. 'Tis many a long year since a maid did come to me for advice and training. I enjoyed the duty. You will often return to us, Maela? I would have thee as companion, for I no longer have a daughter."

"Oh, but you could not keep me away!" Maela assured her. Kissing the older woman's soft, wrinkled cheek, she whispered, "All thanks to thee, Mother Rachel. Indeed, thou art most precious to me!"

Rachel dabbed at tears with her apron. "Now, now! Enough of this. Jonas has gone to the smithy with an ailing horse. He would wish to bid thee farewell."

"I shall not depart until his return. Presently I wish to visit the kittens in the barn again," Maela announced and skipped outside. "When Harry comes, please tell him my whereabouts."

Shortly after noon that day, a courier arrived at Marston Hall. To the surprise of all, he carried a letter, not for any member of the Marston family, but for Harold Jameson, the joiner. Sir David's youngest daughter, Dorcas, delivered the missive to Harry and watched with interest as he broke the seal and opened it.

She saw him stiffen, and all expression erased from his countenance. "Harry, is thy news unwelcome?"

He glanced up. The letter in his hand shook. "Yea, Dorcas, 'tis most unwelcome." He stared blankly at her until the little girl backed slowly from the room and ran to tell her father that Harry was stricken. Never before had she seen Harry without his smile.

Harry struggled to work that day, but in spite of his valiant efforts to keep control of his emotions, his eyes blurred and his hands shook. He spent most of the afternoon sanding and polishing—two tasks that trembling hands could accomplish.

He wanted to see Maela. He needed her. He closed his eyes and was overwhelmed by the memory of her cold, deathlike face and clammy hands. Fear smote him again, and he broke into a cold sweat. Although she had not drowned, Maela might be sick and dying at this moment—she might succumb to a deadly illness, like. . .The tightness in his chest constricted his breathing.

"Harry, lad," a kindly voice startled him. He dropped his cloth and straightened, brushing one hand across his eyes. Sir David Marston stood behind him. "Dorcas has told me of thy letter. 'Tis dire news of thy relations?"

Harry nodded, his eyes upon the floor.

"Alack! My heart sorrows for thee, my friend." He lifted a hand to Harry's shoulder, stretching up a little to reach. "I would do all in my power to aid thee."

Harry nodded again, unable to speak. Finally, he rasped, "Thank you, sir."

"Do you plan to go to your family?"

Harry coughed softly. "Yea. My mother has need of mine aid. I would complete my work here apace, and go to her." He indicated the nearly complete fireplace surround, a masterpiece in walnut, depicting the English countryside.

Sir David's eyes caressed the carved foxes, deer, rabbits, butterflies, trees, and flowers, amazed anew at its intricate detail. "In future, thy name shall be noised abroad as Master Joiner, Harold Jameson. I tremble and stand amazed before thy workmanship."

" 'Tis a gift from God, Sir David, and I must use this gift for His glory and honor. The Holy Scriptures say that to whom much is given, much will be required. 'Tis an awesome responsibility."

"Then God must be greatly pleased with thee, my son. Thy work is masterful, and thy repute beyond praise at the manor. All herein speak of thee with respect and kindness and do marvel at thine impeccable honor. I would know more of thy creed, for mine own satisfies not my soul. I faithfully attend services and hear Scripture read, but, Latin or English, I comprehend it not. I have heard thee relate the Scriptures with alacrity, as though 'tis quick upon thy tongue, and you live the life of a saint with joy. Would you take time to tell me of your faith?"

Sir David drew up two chairs and bade Harry join him. For two hours Harry spoke with him of Jesus, His life, death, and resurrection, and God's power manifested in the daily lives of His people.

"There can be no salvation without Jesus Christ?" Sir David inquired. "What of indulgences, sacraments, and the like? The varied reports between churches oft confuse me. How can a man know which to believe? Men have died for their beliefs on either side, convinced of the truth—yet their beliefs widely differ! How can these things be?"

"I know not, sir. I only know that Jesus claimed, 'I am the way, the truth, and the life. No man comes unto the Father, but by me.' Churches are composed of men, and men can err. God's Word is our sole immutable source of truth. 'Tis by

God's grace we are saved, through faith—and that not of ourselves. It is the gift of God, not of works, lest any man should boast; the apostle Paul wrote these words to the church at Ephesus. Sir, I. . .I would. . ."

Now that he had begun, Harry had second thoughts. What if Sir David betrayed the Puritan believers to the bishop? What if this entire conversation had been a blind, and the nobleman intended to entrap Harry into revealing his compatriots? After all, Sir David himself had appointed the vicar to his position.

*Fear not*, came a gentle Voice within. *Sir David is to be my sheep.*

A strange message, yet clear as though spoken aloud. Harry plunged ahead. "I would invite you to a Bible study. It is composed of brethren who wish to study the Scriptures, share thoughts, and encourage one another in the faith. The meetings are unsanctioned by the vicar and bishop, but there is nothing of sedition in our discussions."

Sir David's clean-shaven face lighted from within. "Indeed?" He bit his lip and stared at the floor, blinking rapidly. "Harry. . .I cannot explain the joy, the hope you have given me. I feel. . .I feel like a starving man which has been offered a feast." He cleared his throat, swallowed hard. "I know the risk you have taken for my sake, and feel the honor of thy confidence. I shall strive to be worthy of thy trust."

He extended his smooth gentleman's hand, and Harry clasped it firmly. The men looked into one another's eyes and were bonded in Christian love.

Harry's heart was still heavy when he left the manor that day, but he was at peace. He had discussed his future with Sir David and felt no anxiety about his imminent departure—the man had been kindness personified, doing all that lay in his power to alleviate Harry's burdens.

Now Harry could think only of Maela. His fears for her had eased, yet he still longed for the sound of her voice, the sight of her loving eyes.

Before heading toward the Fleming farm, Harry stopped by

his cottage for the dogs. They needed a good, long walk. Laitha trotted calmly at his side, while Ragwort darted into every thicket, itching for a good hunt. After spending the day inside the cottage, the terrier was bursting with energy. Dudley vacillated between following Ragwort and sticking close to Harry. The young dog was powerful and fast, yet somewhat timid by nature.

The Fleming barn appeared over a rise, its thatched roof gray with age. Harry scented wood smoke above the blended aromas of plowed fields, new growth, and the early red campion blooming near the tumble of rock wall beside the road, yet the sights and scents gave him little pleasure. Soon he would see Maela. His pace increased.

Harry called out as he approached the house. Maela herself appeared in the barn doorway and returned his wave. His heart lifted; his step quickened. She was well and strong as ever!

Yipping with excitement, Ragwort dashed ahead of Harry. "How now, Ragwort?" Maela called cheerily and bent to greet him.

But Ragwort barreled past her and pounced upon a kitten that had followed her from the barn. Two quick shakes of his head and the kitten went limp.

Maela stood as though frozen. Ragwort dropped the dead kitten and wagged his tail at her, grinning happily.

"Shame, Ragwort!" Harry cried, breaking into a jog. He was too late, but perhaps he could rescue other kittens.

Ragwort's stiff little tail drooped. His ears dropped, and his mouth closed. He looked crushed.

Suddenly, Maela snapped into life. Her hands lifted to clutch her head, and she screeched, "Get thee hence, thou monster! Thou wicked beast! Never shall I forgive thee!" She kicked at the dog, but he dodged, tail between his legs, and ran to Harry for protection.

Harry placed his hand on Maela's arm. She jerked away. "How dare you bring that beast hither? He has slain my favorite kitten! Get thee hence! I do hate the sight of thee!"

She burst into tears, scooped up the crumpled kitten, and rushed, sobbing noisily, into the barn.

Laitha squatted just inside the gate, waiting quietly. Failing to receive consolation from Harry, Ragwort went to her for comfort. She nuzzled him and allowed him to press against her side. Dudley rollicked around them, oblivious to the tense atmosphere.

Harry bowed his head and pinched the bridge of his nose. *Lord, grant me wisdom—and comfort Maela's heart. I know not how to make this right with her.*

Inside the barn, Maela sat upon a bench with the kitten in her lap. She stroked its soft fur, but her eyes stared vacantly across the barn.

Harry stopped before her. He pulled off his cap and fiddled with it. "I cannot tell thee with words of the regret in my heart," he said quietly. "I would help thee bury the cat."

Maela nodded. Harry selected a spade from a peg on the barn wall, knowing Jonas would not mind, and led the way to a corner of Pegasus's pasture. He dug, and Maela watched in silence, shivering with cold. Harry stopped digging long enough to shift his cape to her back. She accepted it, but said nothing. When the hole was deep enough, Maela tenderly laid the kitten to rest. She walked back to the barn while Harry filled the hole and laid stones upon it.

When Harry rejoined her in the barn, she scooted over to give him room on the bench, though she did not look at him. A tear trickled down her cheek; she smeared it with her fist and sniffed. Harry offered her a handkerchief. His lips twitched when she honked her nose into it.

"You should not have brought that dog," she stated coldly. "You know he does hunt small creatures."

"I knew not that he would kill a kitten," Harry admitted.

His gentle tone took some of the starch from her back.

"I hate death, Harry. It is cruel!" She ended in a wail and fresh tears.

Harry said nothing.

Footsteps approached from without, and Jonas entered,

leading a limping cart horse. "Good even, Harry lad. How is it with thee? And Maela, dear maid."

"Well enough, Jonas. And with thee?" Harry rose respectfully, patting the horse's rump as it passed him.

"I find nothing to complain of," Jonas smiled. "God is good. Farley, here, has a bruise on his sole, nothing serious. I was anxious that he was ruined, but all for nothing." He patted the horse's thick chestnut neck. Tethering it in a clean stall, he began to brush it down.

"Harry's dog slew the spotted kitten," Maela told Jonas, like a child in need of a father's condolences.

"I am sorry," Jonas said sincerely. "You may have another as thine own, if you wish it. We lack not for cats."

Maela considered the offer. "I would fear for its safety in the castle. It would find mice aplenty, but I fear that Grandmere's tom would kill it. I think I must leave the kittens here where they can be most happy," she decided regretfully. "Death is cruel, Master Jonas."

He nodded in agreement. "Nevertheless, it is part of life. Until Christ's kingdom returns and He conquers sin and death for all time, we must accept the reality of death in this world. Just as we rejoice at a birth, so we mourn at a death. 'For everything there is a season. . .a time to be born and a time to die.' "

"Is that a quote?"

"Yea, from Ecclesiastes, written by the wise King Solomon. Perhaps at meeting you can hear more of it."

"Mistress Rachel has told me of these meetings."

Harry suddenly turned and walked out of the barn. "Harry, where. . .?" Maela began, but he was gone. She turned her puzzled gaze to Jonas.

"Harry has a sorrow, Maela. You did not observe it?"

"Nay, I was absorbed in. . .mine own sorrow. What is it, Jonas?"

He shook his head. "I know not. You must discover for thyself."

Maela found Harry behind the barn, seated in the bed of a

wagon, elbows propped on his upraised knees, watching horses graze in a back pasture. Hopping up beside him, she scanned his face. He would not meet her gaze. "Harry, tell me thy sorrow, I beg of thee! Forgive my selfish anger—'twas foolish in me, I trow."

He only sighed softly, blowing through his lips. She heard the catch in his breath. Hesitantly she reached out to him, taking his hand in hers. His hand was cold, lumpy with calluses, and very rough to her touch, but she lifted it to her lips and held it between her own warm hands. He must be cold, for she still wore his cloak. That was just like Harry—always thinking of others, never a thought for his own ease.

Harry turned to her, really seeing her for the first time that day. He had seldom beheld her without a cap, and never with clean hair. A gust of wind pushed clouds away from the setting sun, allowing a slender beam to rest upon her head, turning her hair to fire. He sucked in his breath, but had no words to tell her his thoughts.

His free hand reached into his jerkin and pulled out the crumpled letter. Maela released his hand to take it. "This arrived at the hall," he explained shortly.

She read it quickly, giving a horrified cry. "Thy father, thy brother and his wife, and their children—all gone! Oh, my Harry! I wept over a kitten, while you. . . Oh, Harry, can you forgive me?"

Then she was crushed into his arms and felt his entire frame shaking. At first he was silent, but as his grief continued to pour forth, it escaped in racking sobs. Maela had never before heard a man cry—she felt as though her heart would break with his sorrow. She wept with him, wetting his jerkin with her tears while he dampened her neck and shoulder. When his weeping subsided, she wiped her face and his with Harry's handkerchief. It was quite moist by this time.

His reddened eyes and swollen face cut her to the quick. Wishing only to console him, she reached up to pull his head down and kissed his cheeks and his forehead. "Harry, dear one, what shall you do anon?"

"I must repair home. My present work at the hall is nigh completion. I shall finish the surround, then depart. Sir David knows that I must go, for my mother has need of mine aid. He has been exceedingly kind."

"And what of me?" Her voice sounded very small.

"I shall return for thee, Maela; I know not when. I am now the eldest son; after me came five sisters—four yet living—and my eldest brother is but eleven. Mother expects another child in autumn and cannot farm alone. Her father, my grandfather, abides with them, but his strength is limited."

"How long shall you remain here at present?" Seeing him shiver, she removed Harry's cloak, secured it around his shoulders, then crawled beneath it and snuggled against him with only her face peeking out. Almost absently, he wrapped his arm around her shoulders.

"A fortnight, at most. Maela, I would have thee attend church and fellowship with the Flemings. These friends shall support thee during mine absence."

"Mistress Rachel said that she has long besought thee to bring me to worship. Art thou ashamed of me, Harry?"

Put on the spot, Harry floundered. "Ashamed, nay, but. . . afraid. I feared alteration in. . .the special way we are together. . .or were. 'Twas selfish in me, I know." He could not look at her.

"Not selfish, Harry, for I feel the same. I have ever been jealous of thy time and attention."

"We did spoil one another, mayhap," Harry smiled, but felt even more uncomfortable. Their friendship had but rarely included physical contact, and her infrequent caresses had never discomposed him. Could this be the same fearful, wary maid who had shunned any man's touch? Why did she now nestle against his side as though by habit? And why did hot blood rush to his face and disquieting thoughts possess his mind?

"I am thankful for thine introduction to these good Flemings. Mistress Rachel has taught me how to clean my teeth with a broken mint twig and how to dress my hair. Is it not pretty how she has bound it? I am clean everywhere—and I must at last admit the truth in thine assertions that cleanliness is good. I feel. . .wondrous fine. Mistress Rachel sprinkled my hair with rosewater, and she has given me a bottle of mine own."

"Thou art a new creation without as well as within."

"May I come with thee to Lincolnshire?" She sat up straight and looked into his eyes.

Harry could not move. He vividly recalled the warm velvet of her neck, the scented softness of her hair against his face. Heat swept through him, and a frightening desire to take her as wife, come what may. His eyes closed as though in pain. "Greatly though I desire this, it cannot be, Maela."

She stiffened and pushed at his chest. "Mean I nothing to thee?"

He tried to swallow, but could not for the dryness in his throat. "I would not leave thee, but I must! Thou art Sir Hanover Trenton's daughter. Never would he consent to such a match."

"We could marry without his consent," she begged. "We could, Harry! I want nothing more than to be with thee all my life. Surely this is God's will, for He brought us together." She flung her arms around his neck and pressed close.

"We would ever live in hiding. As criminals we would run from the law." Harry held her tenderly. "Thy father would leave no stone unturned, for you have value in his eyes. Should we then be found, I would be hanged, and you would face worse than death. It cannot be so, Maela. Such a life cannot be God's plan for His children. 'Twould be misery, and you would soon learn to hate me for bringing you into it for mine own selfish gain."

"Nay!" she protested into his neck, "Not for thy gain, but for mine! The bishop desires me not as wife, but as his slave! Surely you know. . ." She faltered and stopped.

Rachel's lecture had finally solved some of the puzzles in Maela's brain; not all of these completed puzzles were pleasant to contemplate—such as precisely why the bishop would have her as his slave. But she could not speak of such things to Harry. Realizing how forward her marriage proposal must sound to him, she fell silent, blushing deeply and thankful for the falling dusk.

Harry could only shake his head as he allowed her to pull from his grasp. "We must wait upon the Lord, Maela. He will preserve and defend us in His time. We must not take matters into our hands and attempt to work our plan in His name. Suffering would come of it; of this I am sure."

She drooped. He tried to think of something comforting and loving to say, but his mind was blank. He climbed off the wagon and helped her down. She allowed him to envelop her in his cloak, and they walked back to the house, side by side.

The Flemings invited Harry to remain for the evening meal; afterward he would escort Maela back to the castle. Rachel wished to spend every last minute with Maela, and Jonas absorbed Harry in conversation about biblical principles and obscure Scripture passages.

Lane had wandered over to the manor that night, undoubtedly to visit Lottie. Rachel was delighted with her son's budding romance, for, despite her claims about his popularity, he had always been too shy to court a woman. She and Jonas had nearly given up hope of ever becoming grandparents.

At last Maela stood before the men with a sack of clothing in one hand, a loaded basket in the other. "Rachel has sent a propitiation of biscuits and strawberries to my grandmother, hoping to ease my way. I know not what has occurred in mine absence, but I do know that Grandmere will be angry."

"Thou art prepared at last," Harry observed, rising slowly and smoothing his jerkin. "I thought perhaps Rachel had persuaded thee to remain for aye."

Maela flushed and dropped her gaze to the floorboards. "Verily, I am tempted to remain."

"One last kiss, my child," Rachel requested, folding the girl into her arms. "Come to us if ever you have need."

"I will," Maela agreed. She then hugged Jonas and kissed his leathery cheek. "Extend my farewells to Lane upon his return."

Maela's path from the Fleming's back pasture to the castle was difficult to find in the dark. Harry tripped over hidden obstacles while Maela seemed to glide along like a ghost. He could see her when occasional breaks in the trees allowed moonlight to silver her white cap and face, but her expression was unreadable.

"I have come to the castle only once ere now," he observed, "when you were ill. Remember? 'Twas a stormy night, and cold."

"I recall as though it were last night," she answered. "I feared for thy safety, but God did protect thee."

"I used thy secret tunnel. Do you plan to return hence this night?"

"Nay, I shall walk through the castle door. Mine absence is no secret, and my return must be open or Grandmere shall wax suspicious."

"And Dob?"

"Thou art with me. I fear not Dob with Harry at my side." She sounded both timid and brave. "Grandmere is more to be feared. She did beat me the last time I stayed away overlong. But then I was a child and had no strength." Harry watched her lift her free hand and clench her fist as though to show off powerful muscles. Knowing how slender her arms were, he was not reassured.

"She had best not lay hand to thee while I'm near," Harry muttered grimly. "Come to me straightaway if she tries it." He shifted Rachel's heavy basket of food to his other hand.

"Mistress Rachel has instructed me that I must no longer go alone to thy cottage. It is not seemly, since I am no longer a child."

Harry had feared as much, yet he knew Rachel was right. Unfamiliar feelings now stirred within him, powerful feelings that might prove difficult to control.

"May I visit thee at the castle?"

She immediately shook her head. "I dare not attempt such boldness, Harry. Grandmere would dislike it. I did promise Rachel this day to attend church. I will see thee there, and perhaps we can meet at their home."

She turned and continued on toward the castle. Harry followed in her wake.

A dark blot appeared against the starry sky—the castle keep. Minutes later they stood before the kitchen door. It was locked. Harry pounded with closed fist.

"What shall I say?" Maela squeaked, now that it was too late for planning.

"The truth, though not too much of it," Harry advised.

They heard nothing from within until the door creaked open. "What is it?" Hera Coats asked, holding a candle up to light their faces. "Who are you? We take no lodgers at Castle Trent. Away with you!"

"Grandmere?" Maela quavered.

Hera's bloodshot eyes opened wide. "Ishy? Whatever. . . ? Wherefore came you to be out with this stranger? I did believe thee sick abed!"

The realization that she had not even checked on her granddaughter's health roused Harry's wrath, but he held it in check. The old woman had a gray pallor upon her cheeks. Perhaps she herself had been ill.

"I did fish her out of the river yesterday. The Flemings took her in and cared for her. Mistress Rachel Fleming sends thee greetings, Mistress Coats."

"And these biscuits and berries," Maela added, taking the laden basket from Harry.

Hera's mouth opened and closed a few times. "And how did you come to be in the river, blaggard?" she snapped at Maela.

"I did sneak out," Maela admitted, truthfully enough. "I intended not to fall into the river."

This turn of events had evidently shaken Hera Coats. Reaching out a clawlike hand, she grabbed Maela's arm and dragged her inside. Two berries fell to the floor and rolled into bleak darkness beyond Harry's view. "To thy chamber, wench. I shall settle accounts with thee later."

Then her cold blue eyes pinned Harry to the spot. "What

do you want of the wench? She is not for a commoner—she, the daughter of a great lord. Begone, knave, ere I call the guard."

Thinking of his last clash with "the guard," Harry restrained a bitter smile. He saluted the old woman respectfully, saying, "Fare thee well."

He marched away without a backward glance, though his heart cried many prayers for Maela's protection.

# eleven

*And, lo, I am with you alway, even unto the end of the world.*
Matthew 28:20

" 'They that wait upon the Lord shall renew their strength and mount up with wings as eagles,' " Maela quoted softly as she stood upon a rickety table, leaned both arms upon the narrow windowsill, and gazed across the countryside. "Ever have I loved the prophet Isaiah's words and sought to hide them in my heart. Now they shall comfort me in my sorrow. Jesus is with me always, though Harry cannot be."

Setting her jaw, she stated, "I shall strive to please Jesus with my thoughts and actions. When Harry returns, he shall be pleased with me. I shall attend church and learn more of the Scriptures and of God. My life shall count for Jesus, with or without Harry the joiner." Hopping down from the table, she whisked across the chamber and opened the door with a flourish.

A search through one of her mother's old chests had produced a treasure trove of clothing, scented soap balls, and a tortoiseshell comb and brush set. Maela had nearly grown into her mother's clothing, though the gowns tended to sag in front. Most women possessed but one set of garments; Maela now owned seven, not counting Agnes Fleming's hand-me-downs. This was wealth, indeed.

Now Maela was prepared as though for battle. Clad in one of her mother's embroidered smocks and a puce kirtle and waistcoat, she tied a white cap over her neatly bound braids, hurried downstairs, and marched openly through the kitchen. "Grandmere, I go to church this day. I shall return late." Before Hera could do more than stare in reply, she was gone, running down the road like a deer.

She was too late for the regular church service, but Harry had thought she would prefer the Bible study meeting anyway. It usually took place Sunday afternoon. Master Tompkins, the vicar, seldom audited the doctrine being taught; he preferred his afternoon nap. This was fine with the attending believers; the vicar's sermons contained little meat and tended to lull his flock to sleep.

National church leaders would have frowned heavily upon the meetings being held in the stone church building, but Master Tompkins did not wish to cause trouble, and the bishop was seldom around. Therefore, Trenton parish flourished and grew in knowledge of the Scriptures of its own accord with little fear of reprisal.

People squeezed together on the benches, women on one side, men on the other. A hush fell upon the crowd when Harry entered with Sir David Marston. Many eyes widened, glued to the nobleman's flushed face. Sir David had always attended the liturgical service, never the Bible study. Lane Fleming scooted over to make room and waved to them. Harry nodded his gratitude, and the two men settled upon the bench.

Maela knew Harry had not spotted her, for Rachel sat on the end of their bench, hiding her from view. She had not seen him for three days—it was difficult to keep from peeking around Rachel for a sight of him, especially since his remaining time in Trenton was dwindling rapidly.

The Bible teacher was a wainwright from Cambridge who had come to work in town for a few months, supplying dung carts and a few wagons for the local populace. He opened the huge Bible and began to read aloud from Isaiah. For two hours he read and spoke of God's compassion for His people, of Israel's perfidy, and of God's anger and forgiveness. It was a new passage for Maela, and she soaked up the Scripture with a rapt expression.

Sir David was not the only newcomer to create a stir. Several young girls tried to examine Maela without turning their heads. A few young men were equally interested in the new maiden, casting their eyes across the aisle. Though her bright hair was hidden beneath her cap, her face was sufficient to capture their attention. Maela was unaware of their scrutiny; Rachel noticed and was pleased.

After the service, one of the girls introduced herself as Hepzibah, daughter of the coppersmith. Maela felt shy, but she listened while the other girl chattered, and she soon began to relax. It was another novel experience for her to spend time with girls of her own age. Two other girls soon joined the group. One of them was married and held a baby on her hip. The baby fascinated Maela. She had never seen anything more amazing than this tiny boy with his soft brown curls and dimpled arms. Maela forgot to look for Harry. She forgot everything but the fun of companionship and girlhood.

Sir David was also welcomed into the family of believers. Yeomen, husbandmen, merchants, and craftsmen alike welcomed him as their brother when he professed his faith in Jesus Christ. Days before he had prayed with Harry, committing his life to God's service. Joy radiated from his countenance—none could doubt his sincerity.

While the men talked, Harry watched Maela from across the room as she took the baby from its mother and cuddled it close. She looked mature in her new clothes—too mature. Had Rachel given her that embroidered smock with the scalloped neckline? Harry's fists clenched and relaxed, feeling moist. Such clothing was too old for the child; it drew undue attention to her exquisite neck. He must speak to Rachel about this. . .this impropriety.

Yet it was good to see the girl clean, blooming, happy, healthy. . .lovely. . .and no longer in need of him. He could no longer provide for her, so God had removed her from his hands and placed her, in a sense, with a proper family. It was right and good. So why did he feel as though he had received a fatal wound from a well-driven halberd?

&

"Harry, have you heard about thy little friend? The red-haired maiden—thy fishing companion? Lane tells me she now dwells with his parents." Lottie stopped to chat while dusting the hall.

"Come again?" Harry was sanding down the last portion of his masterpiece—a magnificent red deer, carved with its antlers thrown back, its mouth agape as it bugled a challenge to its foes.

"The maid you rescued from drowning—I cannot recall her name. 'Tis a frightful scandal about town; I cannot believe you have not heard of it. Hera Coats was found dead, and the little maid found sanctuary at the Flemings. Dob Titwhistle has disappeared, and rumor indicates he headed for Parminster Court. The bishop likely enticed him away with higher wages."

Harry decided it was time for a break. Climbing down from the ladder, he picked up his tools. His mind ran in circles.

Lottie followed him to the door. "Lane made this known unto me last evening as we walked out together. Shall you take thy leave soon despite these happenings, Harry? I believed you did love the maid."

"I must repair home. My family depends upon me." Harry felt like tearing out his hair. This exigency would surely bring Lord Trenton to his castle in a hurry, and then what would become of Maela? She was now "ripe" enough to tempt even the bishop.

He could not deny his hurt that Maela had run to the Flemings for aid, not to him. And yet, it served him right. He would soon be leaving her in her time of great need.

Harry simply told Master Lyttleton, "I have emergency business of a personal nature. The carvings will be complete tomorrow as planned." And he left.

It was a cool, dismal morning. Fog lay thickly in shallow vales and drifted haphazardly across the road. At times, Harry could scarcely see his hand before his face. He felt his spirits drooping and fought to keep them high.

The Fleming farm looked deserted and dreary, though smoke trickled from the chimney. Pegasus grazed near the roadside fence; he spotted Harry and whickered a friendly greeting. Harry took a moment to ruffle the pony's thick mane. Pegasus was getting older, like Samson. His face was sprinkled with white hair.

Another horse joined them at the fence, hoping for a treat. It was an immense gray, dappled beneath and nearly white above. Its mane and tail were dark at the roots and white at the ends. Heavy white feathering made boots around its black feet. Its skin was dark gray, and its eyes looked very dark upon that white face. Harry had never seen such a horse—the top of his head scarcely reached its withers. Its coloring was unusual and quite handsome.

"That gelding shall be thine," Jonas said from behind him, making Harry start.

"Indeed! I have not the means to pay for such a beast. It looks strong enough to pull thy barn from its foundation. It must stand eighteen hands!"

"Verily, it is strong indeed, but contrary, high-spirited, and ever hungry. My Suffolk horses pull well enough, are calm in spirit, amenable, and eat half as much. I must let this fine beast go. I bought it at market some months past, captured by its handsome face and impressive muscle, though it was in poor condition at the time. Not a se'ennight passed ere I knew 'twas a mistake. Its will is as strong as its neck, and it cares not to pull a plow. Even Lane confessed himself out of patience with the beast."

"And it is to be mine for the agreed upon price?" Harry could scarcely believe his luck. "It has the aspect of a war horse, a charger."

"No doubt that was its origin."

"Is it broken to saddle?"

"Yea. Should it displease thee, thou mayest freely choose another. I would not cheat thee, Harry."

"I know that. I trust thy judgment, Jonas." Harry patted the horse's shoulder and suddenly remembered. "Maela! Is she here with thee?"

"She is in the barn," Jonas answered simply. "You did come to see her?"

"Has she departed the castle for aye?"

"I know not. Only that she came to us in her need, and we shall keep her while we may. Do you wish to ride the horse? Its saddle is in the barn. I will prepare it for thee."

Harry couldn't resist. "If you would."

Jonas walked with Harry to the barn and picked out a large head collar. "I shall call when he is saddled."

Harry nodded and waited for Jonas to leave before inquiring, "Maela, where art thou?" There was no sign of the girl.

"In the loft."

Harry jumped, caught the edge of the loft opening with his fingers, and easily hauled himself up. He waited for his eyes to adjust to the dark. Something scurried amid the mounds of hay. There was a thump, a squeak, and a large tabby cat appeared along the wall with something dangling from its mouth.

"Is that the mother of thy kittens?" he asked.

"It is the father, I believe," a quiet voice replied from his left.

"I did not bring the dogs with me this time."

She didn't answer, so he went on, "I heard of thy grandmother's death. Lottie told me this morn. I came straightaway to find thee."

She crawled toward him slowly, for her smock entangled her legs. Her kirtle was looped up and tucked into her leather belt. Harry crawled to meet her and pulled her close. She clutched his jerkin and sighed.

"I must learn to survive without thee, Harry, but it is hard."

"Tell me."

Maela's low voice trembled. "Grandmere went outside. I heard her shout and Dob shout, and then silence. I suspected no tragedy, for they often fight. But then I heard Dob enter the castle—he has entered it not since she laid the curse. Somehow I knew then that she was dead. She has been ill, but I knew not that her death was near. I ran and hid myself until Dob quit searching and calling for me. Then I packed up my raiment and fled here. I wanted thee, Harry, but. . .I may not have thee."

"Maela," Harry blurted in dismay. "I am ever thy friend!

Conceal not thy troubles from me."

Jonas called from below. "Thy horse awaits, Harry."

"Thy horse?" Maela echoed.

"Perhaps. We shall see if it will be my horse. I must not make Jonas wait." He swung himself down from the loft, then waited for Maela to follow.

She peered shyly down at him. "Away, Harry. I shall follow in my turn."

"I would assist thee. Come," he beckoned, reaching up for her.

She slipped her legs over the edge, trying to keep them modestly covered. Hesitating again, she asked, "Art thou certain? I am heavy."

"Thou art a feather," Harry insisted, wriggling his fingers at her.

She jumped before he was ready. He caught her, but staggered backward. She began to giggle, her face pressed against his chest. "Staggered by a feather," she mocked.

"I would see thee do better!" he protested. "You shall catch me the next time." He hugged her tighter. His brows contracted; he touched her cheek gently, but he only said, "Come and see my horse."

Catching her by the hand, he dragged her outside toward the gelding, which pawed the ground with a hoof the diameter of Maela's head. She pulled her hand away and retreated to the barn doorway.

"The giant gray," she breathed in awe. "Can you ride such a horse, Harry? Have you ridden before?"

"I have oft ridden, but I shall not know whether I can ride this horse until I try it." Harry took the horse's reins, put his foot in the stirrup, and leaped lightly into the saddle.

The horse danced in place, an impressive sight. Its neck, shoulders, and haunches bulged with muscle, and its mouth gaped and slavered as it champed the bit. It snorted and shook and rattled its tack, making far more noise than Maela liked.

Harry's face shone with excitement and pleasure. To Maela's surprise, he apparently enjoyed this display. He slapped the animal's neck and laughed aloud. "Grand fellow!"

"I would advise thee to ride first within the pasture," Jonas said calmly, opening the gate for Harry and the horse.

Harry guided the horse through the gate, then gave it rein and requested more speed. The great horse nearly reared as it leaped into motion. With the sound of thunder it pounded across the field. Harry's hat flew off; his hair lifted in the breeze. The pair disappeared into the fog.

Maela looked at Jonas. He smiled. "Fear not, child. Harry manages the beast well. I was not certain of this horse for him, but now I know that it will do."

The earth shook, and horse and rider loomed out of the fog. "Would you ride with me, Maela?" Harry asked. His eyes were sparkling. Every white tooth in his mouth showed through his dark beard when he smiled.

Maela hesitated, looking at that awesome creature. But when her eyes returned to Harry's, she could only nod. He reached down, Jonas boosted her up, and she flew to the horse's back. They were off again, racing through the silvery mists. The pasture sloped slightly downward. Maela wrapped her arms tightly around Harry's waist, closed her eyes, and hid her face between his shoulder blades.

"He is incredibly strong," Harry exulted. "He notices not thy weight. To him, you truly are a feather!"

"What will you call him?" Maela shouted, then gulped when the horse hopped over a small ravine.

"I have not decided. Do you like him?"

"I prefer my Pegasus."

She felt Harry's chuckle. He slowed the horse to a walk. Maela could scarcely believe how wide her legs had to stretch to straddle its vast back. She was going to be sore after this ride.

"I never dreamed that I should possess such a beast. He shall carry me to Lincoln within three days! He is not so very fast, but ever so strong. He will never tire, I believe."

A great knot formed in Maela's chest. It had become a familiar knot during these past weeks, forming whenever thoughts of Harry's departure recurred.

"Thursday, I head north," Harry told her bluntly. "I would not leave thee, but I have no choice. I shall return as soon as ever I may. You may write to me. I will write to thee."

"I know not whereof to write, and I know not how to send a letter."

"Jonas would arrange delivery for thee, I am certain. Write to me of Samson, Pegasus, the hens, and the goats. Tell me of Dudley, for I shall leave him here to protect thee. Tell of thy meetings with the brethren, of friends you have made. I would know thy thoughts and feelings, as ever, and I would share mine own with thee. I would tell thee of Laitha and Ragwort and of this horse."

"Saul."

"Come again?"

"I suggest the name King Saul, for thy horse stands head and shoulders above his fellows."

Harry laughed. "Indeed he does. I accept thy suggestion with gratitude. Saul he shall be from this moment."

He leaned forward and slapped the horse's shoulder. "Saul, my fine fellow, we shall return to the barn now, if you please." He nudged the horse's sensitive sides, and King Saul obligingly burst into a rapid trot.

"Oof," Maela protested, so Harry asked for a canter. Saul shifted his bulk into a higher gear, and the ride smoothed dramatically.

Wednesday afternoon, Harry collected his pay and took leave of Sir David Marston, his family, and the servants. He was gratified by the sorrow shown on his behalf.

"If ever you return to Suffolk, my house is open to thee—our finest guest room for my beloved brother in Christ. No fee, no honor can repay the debt I owe thee, my friend."

Harry flushed, abashed. Sir David chuckled, shaking his hand vigorously. "Or, should you prefer, we shall find work for thee, Harry. Lady Sarah desires a carved bedstead."

"Indeed, I do, Harry!" his wife agreed.

"The coppice cottage shall ever be open for thy use—you have improved it beyond measure during thy tenure."

"I am hopeful of return, sir, and I thank thee for thy surpassing kindness. 'Twas an honor to serve thee. God bless thee and thy house."

"Return to us quickly, Harry!" little Dorcas called.

George, Lottie, Simon, and others of Harry's friends were equally sorry to see him go. He was touched by their kind words and wishes for his return. He had never before realized how many friends he possessed at the manor.

He cleaned out the cottage and closed its door for the last time. The roses climbing around its door were budding; in a day or two they would burst into color. Maela's flower garden would be desolate this year; the kitchen garden would fill with weeds. A lump caught in Harry's throat as memories flooded over him: Maela lying before the fire with her head on Laitha's back, milking Genevieve, laboring in her garden, romping with Ragwort, toasting bread and cheese over the fire. Together, he and Maela had turned this old cottage into a home. He was sorry to leave it.

That night he sat before another fireplace in a ladder-backed chair that creaked ominously beneath his weight. His hands, for once, idle, he stared into the fire, his mind busily mapping out his route to Lincolnshire. Because he must skirt the marshy fens and good roads were infrequent, he estimated three long or four shorter travel days. Considering Saul's stamina and strength, Harry hoped for three days.

Maela sat at Harry's feet with Ragwort in her lap; she and the dog had reconciled days before. Dudley curled around her bottom like a pillow, his long head on Harry's foot. Laitha lay stretched upon the hearth, kicking slightly in her sleep. Rachel and Jonas also sat before the fire—Rachel knitting, Jonas polishing tools. Lane was out with Lottie again.

As the fire crackled, Maela's hair shimmered like an autumn wood in sunlight. Harry's eyes rested upon it. She yawned and stretched. Harry's eyes followed her every move.

"At what time shall you take your leave come the morn, Harry?" Rachel asked abruptly.

"I set out ere dawn. I shall try to make Cambridge on the

morrow, Stamford the second day, and home, nigh Scamblesby, the third evening."

"I packed a bag of food for thee, bread, bacon, fruit, vegetables, and the like. Plenty to last thee a day or two. Have you fodder for the horse?"

"Jonas has seen to that."

Rachel shook her head sadly. "Maela shall pine for thee, I doubt not."

"And I shall sadly miss her company." Again he looked down at the girl. Long lashes fluttered against her pale cheeks. She would not look at him.

"You shall have thy family and many other young companions to fill your need of fellowship, as shall Maela. Now as to accommodations this night; Lane will share his bedchamber, or you may repose here upon the kitchen hearth. The sitting room is chill."

"This hearth is adequate for my needs."

Rachel nodded. "I shall find thee a blanket."

Maela gently put Ragwort from her lap, rose, and walked to the ladder. Without a backward glance or word, she climbed to her loft bedroom. Harry watched until she disappeared into the darkness, then turned puzzled eyes upon Rachel. Why was Maela forever leaving him alone with no explanation?

Rachel only smiled, then rose to find the promised quilt.

Harry lay awake long after the couvre-feu, the metal dome that protected embers during the night, was in place, and everyone else in the house had retired. He had rolled up his cape to pillow his head. Laitha and Dudley lay full length against his sides, snoring softly. Ragwort curled between his feet.

A rustle came from the loft. Harry thought he saw movement at the top of the loft ladder, but thick darkness made him uncertain. Stealthy footsteps confirmed his suspicion. Maela was climbing down. Did she need to use the jakes?

Her feet padded softly in the fresh reed matting. Harry saw her as a dim white figure approaching. His stomach clenched into a tight knot.

"Maela?" His whisper made no sound.

She knelt down beside him. Laitha whimpered and sat up, placing her paw in Maela's lap. Maela wrapped her arm around the dog and bade her hush.

"I could not let thee depart without a word, Harry." She leaned close. Harry caught the scent of roses. "I could not look at thee this night lest my tears begin to flow, for I fear that I shall not look upon thy face again until we meet in heaven. Thou art my greatest blessing next to Jesus Christ, and I will love thee ever. I shall pray for thee each day that I draw breath; and if you wed another, I shall endeavor to love her as a sister though my heart does break."

Harry tried desperately to think of a calm, controlled answer; but when Maela's soft lips touched his forehead, he could not check his startled gasp.

She jerked away, staring at him. "Harry, I thought you did slumber!"

He sat up, dropped his face upon his upraised knees, and groaned, "Would that I did."

Maela wept softly into Laitha's shoulder. Silence stretched long. At length, she returned to her loft bedroom.

Harry lay awake for a long time. *Lord, I need Thy comfort and strength, for my heart is sore afflicted!*

Harry's departure seemed almost anticlimactic. After helping Lane, Jonas, and the hireling with the morning chores, Harry ate heartily of Rachel's wheat cakes and honey, fried salt pork, dried fig compote, and fresh milk. Rachel had insisted that he take a meal before departing. She bustled about at the fire, rosy and bright no matter the hour.

Maela did not appear until Harry had nearly finished eating. When she did clamber down her ladder, she looked as though she had been crying throughout the night. Her eyelids were swollen, her cheeks blotched. Hair had pulled loose from her frazzled braid and dangled around her face.

She looked desperate until her eyes lighted upon Harry. "Oh, I feared you had gone and I had missed you!" she gasped. Her hand quickly covered her lips, and color crept into her cheeks.

Harry gulped a bite of wheat cake without chewing it well enough. It hurt all the way down. He took a drink of milk and wiped his mustache with the back of his hand. "Would I depart and not bid you farewell?" he growled. "What manner of man do you consider me, Maela?"

She looked abashed. "I did but fear it in my dreams, Harry."

It was time to leave. Rising, Harry thanked Rachel and Jonas for the lodging and board. "You are kind friends indeed," he said haltingly. "A man could not ask for better. I cannot tell you how thankful I am that Maela may stay here at your house."

"Thy horse awaits thee at the gate," Lane said from the doorway. He had saddled King Saul while Harry ate.

"Let us ask the Lord's blessing upon thy journey," Jonas suggested.

They joined hands in a circle and bowed their heads as Jonas requested God's traveling mercies for Harry. Maela's little hand was cold in Harry's grasp.

"All thanks to thee, Brother Jonas," Harry heartily shook Jonas's hand, then embraced him. "I shall miss thy quiet wisdom and generous nature."

Lane shook his hand. "God give thee good journey, Harry."

"Harry, my boy!" Rachel hugged him. She was very soft in his arms, like a warm, living feather pillow. Tears trickled down her round cheeks as she backed away. "Come back to us."

Harry felt tender toward her. "Mistress Rachel," he said softly. "I honor thy kind heart."

Maela held back at first, but when Harry looked lovingly at her, she threw herself into his arms and sobbed. Her held her close and pressed a kiss upon her head. "I shall love thee always, Maela."

# twelve

*Wait for the Lord: be strong and take heart
and wait for the Lord.*
Psalm 27:14 (NIV)

"Thou art lost in thy mind again, Harry," Rosalind Jameson
chided her older brother. "Do you dream of your beloved?"

Harry blinked and resumed scratching Ragwort's back.
"Perhaps," he allowed. He sat upon the doorstep, looking out
at rolling hills. It was mild for November. Evening sunlight
streamed across the hilltops, leaving the vales in shadow.

"In your mind, you do kiss her and touch her soft skin?"
the girl teased unmercifully. Rosalind was lately betrothed to
a local tanner, and her mind was consumed by thoughts of
romance. Harry often found her company tiresome.

"Rosalind!" their mother intervened. "Have done! Harry
pines after the damsel enough without thy taunts to remind
him of her. I would have thee finish the laundering, maiden.
Thine idle hands give me no aid."

Standing in the doorway, Susan Jameson smoothed her
apron over her shrinking belly. Her baby boy was now a
month old, bringing the total of living Jameson children to
nine. Four had died in childhood, and Horace, the eldest, just
last winter, along with his wife and two children.

Even more difficult to bear was the absence of her beloved
husband, Rolf Jameson, born Raoul Inigo Diego de la
Trienta. Only days before their twenty-fourth wedding
anniversary, he had dropped dead in the field while sowing
corn. Yet the Lord had given Susan a joy to ease the sorrow
of great loss—baby Rolf was the picture of his handsome
Spanish father.

Turning up a pert nose at her older brother, Rosalind flounced off toward the river. Harry found it difficult to believe that his sister would soon be wed. She was younger than Maela and seemed too immature to consider marriage, though her pretty face and figure attracted hordes of admirers.

"What news weighs heavy on thy mind, my son?" Susan sat beside him on the step.

He glanced sideways at her. "News from London. Nothing to concern thee, Mother."

"If it brings this scowl to thy face, it concerns me."

Harry smiled acknowledgment, though his eyes remained worried. "I hear that Sir Hanover Trenton has fallen from grace. It is noised abroad that he made adulterous dalliance with one of the queen's ladies-of-honor, and Her Majesty is justifiably furious."

"And?"

"He has disappeared, most likely to the continent. There is a reward for his capture. I expect he would face the block."

"Wherefore does this hapless nobleman's plight bring a scowl to thy face, Harry? You have minded little the executions of other nobles."

Harry sighed. "He is Maela's father."

"Thy Maela? The maiden you love to such distraction?"

He nodded.

Susan blinked rapidly in surprise. "You have temerity indeed to aspire to a nobleman's daughter. Why did you keep these particulars hidden from me these many months?"

"She is his natural daughter, Mother. He cares for nothing but the profit she may bring him. And I purposed not to conceal the matter; 'tis simply that thy mind has been occupied with more pressing matters than one son's marriage plans."

His mother pondered in silence, far from pleased, but unwilling to hurt Harry. "She has written thee, I recall, but not since summer. Have you proposed matrimony? Are you certain quite that she has no plan to wed another? Her father might already have contracted a match."

"Maela would ne'er consent to wed another, and I cannot

but think that friends would have sent me word had the bish—" He broke off, then resumed, "I hope that soon Maela shall be my wife."

Susan reached a work-worn hand to touch his hair. "I would have thee near me, Harold, but I would rather have thee content with thy lot. You have left all in order to aid your kin; you have given freely of your strength and skill for our benefit while enduring thine own loneliness. We can now survive a short season without thee, for the fields are harvested, the sheep marketed or pastured, and all is well in hand. I believe the Lord shall richly reward thee for thy faithful labor and patience. You shall ride forthwith, settle thine affairs, and return with thy bride ere the new year begins."

He glimpsed a twinkle in her eye as she gripped his upper arm. Her two hands together could not half span it. "Thou art grown soft and lazy from dreaming of thy love."

Harry couldn't help but smile. He looked into his mother's blue eyes and saw her pride and love for him. "You will love her, Mother. She is. . .very dear."

Susan leaned against her son and reached up to stroke his neatly trimmed beard. "I shall love her because you love her. When will you depart?"

"Soon." He wrapped his arm around her and squeezed gently. She was a sturdy woman, but to Harry she felt little and soft. Strange, that his mother should seem small when she had once cradled him in her arms. "I shall not keep long from thee again, Mother."

"I know. You have a tender spirit toward women, as do few among men. You are akin to thy father, and you well know how I did love him!"

"That I do know." Harry pressed a kiss upon his mother's forehead.

❧

"Is Lottie not a comely bride?" Hepzibah Wheeler asked, tossing rice at the newlyweds as they climbed into the rented carriage.

"In truth, she is. Her gown matches her eyes and shows her

hair to advantage," Maela answered warmly. "Lane adores her, and his parents greatly approve the match."

"We thought Lane Fleming would never wed. Many did attempt to catch his eye, but no maid could bring him to speak!" Elizabeth Goddard giggled, shifting her toddler higher on one hip. "It needed Lottie to snare him—a maid both bold and unabashed!"

"Will you remain at their house? I know you are friendly with Lottie, but. . ." Prudence Foster held her pregnant belly with both hands. "I would little desire an unwed maid in my household."

"Prudence, that is unkind!" Elizabeth chided. "Lottie is not jealous of Maela, I am certain. They have regard one for another."

"Nevertheless, were I Lottie, I would place no other maid before my husband's eyes—at least for a season or two. What has become of the joiner? We did all believe he would wed thee, Maela, but it appears his attraction was fleeting." Prudence's pale blue eyes held little warmth.

Blood rushed into Maela's face. "I received a letter from him only a fortnight past. He shall return for me." Her voice sounded tight.

"I am certain he shall," Elizabeth soothed. "Harry was besotted with Maela, Pru, and no wonder, for she is gentle, good, and surpassing fair. Make no doubt, he will return as soon as ever he can." The plump, kindly girl-mother patted Maela's arm.

"Hmph!" Prudence gave Maela a disdainful glance and picked her way down the church steps.

Once she had passed out of earshot, Elizabeth said, "Prudence is only jealous, dearest. Thy Harry never gave her a second glance, and she did esteem him greatly. She wed Clarence Foster as second choice, and he does not make her happy."

"Make haste, or we shall miss the procession," Hepzibah reminded them. "Lottie's brother carries the cake, though I fear he has too oft partaken from the bride's cup!"

Leading the wedding guests into town, Melvin Putnam followed after the bridal carriage, bearing the heavy cake on a great platter atop a short pole. The crowd gasped in horror as he reeled, nearly impaling the cake upon a tree limb. The portly young husbandman did, indeed, appear cheerfully drunk.

" 'Twill be a miracle if we taste that cake," Elizabeth remarked as she started down the steps. "I believe 'tis not long for this world."

"I care little." Hepzibah lifted her kirtle and skipped down the steps. "Dancing shall continue, with or without wedding cake. I shall dance every dance with Joseph Clark this night!"

"The next wedding party shall likely be thine, Hepzibah," Elizabeth smiled at the exuberant girl. The three young women had been friends their entire lives, and Maela appreciated the generous way they had allowed her into their circle.

"Join us, Maela? We shall be jolly the whole night through!"

"Nay, though I thank thee. I shall remain." Her eyes followed the chattering, giggling women, but she felt no desire to join the procession. Dancing held no attraction, and the thought of plum cake made her feel ill. Prudence's thrust had sunk deep into Maela's tender spirit.

When no one was looking, Maela wandered across the churchyard, threading her way between gravestones. Her mother's grave was not here, and neither was her grandmother's. They had both been buried in a common graveyard on the outskirts of town, with beggars, criminals, and other no-accounts. Maela stepped over a stile and kept walking. She missed Dudley. He was usually with her, but not today, not during a wedding.

"Lord God," she prayed under her breath, walking faster and faster. "I have striven daily to surrender my life into Thy hands. I long to be the woman You have created me to be, yet I fail dismally. Ever within my heart is an ache, a longing for Harry. Shall it ever be so? Must I give up my desire to be his wife?"

Tears overflowed as she walked and prayed, wrestling with God. At last, she groaned, "I will surrender him, Lord, but I must have Thy love to take his place. I cannot live without love!"

Blindly she walked, not knowing whither her steps led. "Rachel and Jonas love me, as do Lane, Lottie, and other friends, but they can do very well without me. I want someone to love who needs me, Father! I want Harry. . .but more than anything I yearn to be used of Thee to bring about Thy will on this earth."

She was obliged to stop, for a stream blocked her way. Glancing around, she realized that she was thoroughly lost. This did not distress her, for she knew the area well. *I need only find a clearing, look for the castle, and I shall be oriented.*

A strange feeling crept over her—the feeling of being watched. Wise in woodcraft, Maela dropped to the ground and tried to slide into the bushes, but rapid, crunching footsteps told her she was too late. She tried to scramble to her feet, but a hard hand clapped over her mouth, and she was bodily lifted from the ground. "Silence, or I shall slit thy throat."

She nodded, and the hands loosened. Her assailant gripped her shoulders, turned her about, and Maela gasped, "Lord Trenton!"

"Ishy?" Shock turned his dirty face gray. "I did not know thee!" He released her so roughly that she staggered. Striding away, he seemed lost in thought. Then he turned, a smile spreading across his face. "I thought thee dead or gone away. 'Tis a pleasure, indeed, to find thee well and. . ." he gave her an assessing look, "in remarkable appearance. You have truly ripened into a peach!" He chuckled at the old joke.

"We envisioned thee escaped to the continent, sir. There has been no sign of thee, though the queen's soldiers search diligently." Maela's feelings concerning his return were jumbled. She was thankful to see him alive and well, but not here.

"Have you heard from the bishop?"

She shook her head warily. "Not for many months. Is he yet friend to thee?"

He chuckled grimly. "He should be, for his hand was deeply in the pie along with mine. His head shall roll alongside mine if I go to the block!"

Maela shuddered. "Is the queen also angry with him?"

"Nay. Her Majesty knows only of my part in the matter, not of his. The silly trollop admires him and said nothing to the queen of his guilt—only of mine."

Though she pitied Trenton's plight, Maela's heart lightened at this news. Perhaps she need no longer fear Bishop Carmichael. Should Harry return, they could marry and be free of worry. Her father was in no position to object.

"Come." Trenton gripped her arm and dragged her along behind him.

"Where are you taking me?" she cried in alarm.

Minutes later, she discovered for herself. Taking Maela straight to the opening of her hidden tunnel, he climbed down and dragged her, stumbling and panting, after him into the darkness. Instead of entering the great hall, he opened the door in the side of the tunnel and pushed her in before him. Immediately, she blundered upon a short, steep flight of steps. Climbing, she was surprised to find that the passageway was not completely dark. Small slits let in daylight from high above. She seemed to be in a very narrow passageway within the castle wall.

At the far end of the corridor, Hanover opened another door and shoved Maela inside. Without another word, he closed the door and latched it from his side. His footsteps died away.

Horrified, Maela stared at her dim surroundings. Large casks lined the walls of the chamber. She tried to figure out exactly where she was in relation to the castle, and decided she must be somewhere near the great hall or the entry hall and on a level with the dungeons.

The only way to be certain was to look out one of those air vents. How could it be that she had never noticed them during all her years of exploring the castle? She clambered to the top of one row of casks and peered through a crack. Only dirt lay before her. She tried to get a better view, but the horizontal slit was angled down.

She tried the other side of the chamber. These "windows" gave her a view of flagstone flooring, but at least she could see a few feet to another wall. This must be the entry hall. It was dimly lighted, as an indoor hall would be. Her guess had been accurate.

Maela paced the floor until her feet ached. Would anyone notice her absence during the bustle of wedding celebrations? It was highly unlikely.

At last she heard her father at the door. He entered, carrying a rushlight holder, blankets, and a laden sack. Maela's heart sank. It looked as though she was to be a prisoner here.

"But why? Wherefore hold me captive?"

"You are my means of escape. I was obliged to fly from London with little blunt, and had no means of obtaining enough to purchase my passage. My wife would gladly hand me over for trial, and I have nothing to offer in exchange for aid. Titus shall pay handsomely for thee, as agreed upon many years since, and subsequently I shall arrange passage to Calais." He seemed smugly pleased with himself.

Yet, for the first time, Maela noticed how threadbare his clothing was. His recent trials had marked his face and grayed his hair. He looked the part of a wanted and desperate man.

"How will you notify the bishop of your plans?"

"He shall come. I know Titus well, and he shall come after thee. He is. . .insatiable."

Maela shuddered. The bishop's burning eyes were fresh in her memory.

Trenton made two more trips, bringing fresh water, a chamber pot, and a straw pallet. "At night I shall allow thee to walk about the castle, to wash and perhaps cook, but the risk is too great in daylight."

"Where do you lodge?"

"In finer quarters than these," he grumbled, "yet ill fitting my station. It suits me to have conversation with thee; mine own company grows tedious. You shall tell me what has come to pass here, for I confess myself amazed at the changes wrought in mine absence. Where is the witch? And that toad, Dob Titwhistle? He owes me a considerable sum, and I descry no hint of his whereabouts. I did arrive to find my castle deserted, my holdings unguarded. Even the stables and outbuildings stand empty! Why has neither word nor payment come to me since spring?"

Maela sighed. *Lord, what is Thy purpose in bringing me here? I asked Thee for someone who desperately needs my love, but this is not the answer I did envision.*

# thirteen

*And he said unto me, My grace is sufficient for thee:*
*for my strength is made perfect in weakness.*
2 Corinthians 12:9

"Whoa, Saul," Harry reined in his horse before the gates of Marston Hall. It seemed strange to be back after nearly seven months' absence. "Do you recall this place?" he asked the dogs. Ragwort perched before him on the saddle. The little fellow's legs had long since given out.

Harry clucked and nudged Saul's sides. Marston's dogs rushed to meet them as they entered the drive. Laitha was quickly surrounded by old acquaintances, and Ragwort barked greetings from his perch. Tired as he was, King Saul shied and bucked a little while dogs swarmed about his legs.

"Harry!" a young boy shouted in excitement as Harry neared the stables. "You have returned! We nigh despaired to behold thee again."

"Well met, Ned," Harry called back. "Come, hold my horse, and I shall reward thy courage. Saul is kindly, though the dogs have made him mettlesome."

The boy took Saul's rein as Harry swung from the saddle. "Shall I walk him for thee, Harry?"

"Yea, and give him drink when he has cooled. Thou art a good lad, Neddy." Harry thumped the boy companionably on the shoulder.

Word of Harry's arrival spread like ripples on a pond. Before he had even reached the house, Sir David burst from its doors. "Harry! Harry Jameson! How is it with thee, son? I have craved the sight of thy face these many months, but had begun to believe you would never return." He gripped

Harry's hand heartily, clapping him on the arm. "Enter, sir, and welcome."

Harry followed his former master through the great front doors and into a parlor. "I came first to see thee, sir. I have just ridden into town and would ask—"

"Has noise of Lord Trenton's disgrace traveled even unto Lincolnshire? 'Tis a sad business. Hanover was my friend, though we seldom spoke these many years. And now this disappearance of his natural daughter! I know she was thy particular friend, so—"

"What is this?" Harry demanded, stiffening. "What of Maela?"

"Ah! You had not heard? I am indeed sorry to bear these tidings. The maiden disappeared nearly a month since. She attended the nuptial celebration of her friends, Lane Fleming and my former housemaid Lottie. Afterward, she vanished and has not been seen since. They set dogs upon her trail, but it had rained and frosted in the night, and the trail was cold."

Harry's face was ashen. His thoughts ran wild.

Sir David was still speaking. "Were I not a Christian, I would believe the Trenton line cursed. First the son's death, then Hanover's title and holdings stripped from him. Now the maiden has disappeared. The castle is a ruin, and the tenants pay no rent since that crook absconded—what was his name?"

"Dobbin Titwhistle. Trenton's son has perished?"

"They know not what took the lad. It came of a sudden. One day he was in health, the next, gravely ill. He had fits and spasms, they say, and went rigid. The mother said the lad had trodden upon a horseshoe clamp some days before and punctured his foot deepiy; but the wound had healed and the doctor thought all was well. They leeched and drenched him, but to no avail. 'Twas a sad business, from start to end."

Harry was only half listening.

"I must find Maela. I ask, sir, for use of the coppice cottage. I would pay its rent."

"Nay, it is thine to use, Harry. It stands vacant. These

calamities have stricken thee a mighty blow, I can see. I sorrow for thee, my son. Thou art foremost in my prayers until thy maid is found safe. I would do anything to aid thee; if thou hast need, come to me."

Harry expressed his appreciation and soon took his leave.

The cottage looked neglected and lonely. Harry realized in one glance that its small paddock and shed would never do for King Saul. He must find other accommodations for the horse. The cottage also seemed small and dreadfully empty. Excited, Laitha and Ragwort inspected every corner, sneezing at intervals. Ragwort killed a rat near the chicken coop. He tossed and caught it cheerfully.

Leaving his pack on the dusty bench, Harry hurried back out to his waiting horse. Saul had rested at Marston Hall; he was ready for a good canter. His great hooves splatted in the road's muddy ruts. Laitha loped nearby on the grassy verge. Ragwort stood before Harry on the saddle, his small forepaws planted upon Saul's crest, his black nose drinking in scents. Harry held him by the tail.

The Fleming farm looked neat and prosperous, as always. A sizable addition had been built on one side of the house, undoubtedly for Lane and his new bride. Jonas appeared in the barn doorway.

"Jonas!" Harry shouted, waving an arm over his head as Saul trotted up the lane.

Jonas returned Harry's wave with vigor.

The two men met in the barnyard. Harry swung down from Saul's back and clasped Jonas's arm, then hugged him. The older man's blue eyes sparkled with pleasure. Turning to the horse, he slapped Saul's sweaty neck and said, typically, "The gelding looks well. He has served thee faithfully?"

"There can be no better horse. He desires a good rubdown and—nay, Jonas, I shall care for him. I did not intend that you should do my work," he tried to protest, but Jonas waved him off, leading the horse toward the barn.

"I shall tend him. Go to Rachel in the house, lad. We have much to tell thee. I shall join you shortly."

Ordering his dogs to follow, Harry headed for the house, his cape swirling behind him in a stiff breeze. Rachel burst into raptures at the sight of him, laughing, hugging him, and wringing her pudgy hands in turn. She dragged him into the house; he bumped his head on the lintel. "Dogs, come as well," she invited the animals. "Does your head ache, Harry? Let me take your hat and cape, sir. I say 'sir' for you have changed so these months. Tush! You even have a sword! Have you been in a duel?"

"Nay, I did carry it for defense upon the road," Harry tried to explain, but she scarcely paused for breath.

" 'Tis a grand man thou art, Harry Jameson! I had forgotten thy vastness—thou art as tall as Lane and twice his magnitude. Sit here now. You have increased while you were away, though I detect no fat upon thee." She prodded his thick chest muscles and flat stomach as she spoke. Harry meekly allowed her motherly inspection, thankful to have no audience. His dogs settled upon the hearth, panting audibly.

Rachel continued her inspection. "They have fed thee well and worked thee hard. Thine arms are of bronze, and hairy as Esau's. Thy trim little beard resembles that of a high lord. Maela shall—oh!" Distressed, she clapped one hand over her mouth.

"I have been apprised of her disappearance. If you would, relate to me the facts."

"Oh, if only you had come sooner, mayhap the child would yet be here! 'Twas the morning after Lane's wedding—did you hear of it? Lane did wed Lot—"

"I did hear of it. 'Tis glad tidings, indeed. What of Maela?"

"She did not attend the festivities; her friends saw her last at the church. Jonas raked the countryside for her, and our brethren searched likewise. Nothing has been seen of her."

"The castle?" Harry's voice was deadly calm.

"It is deserted. They have searched it, to no avail."

"Where is Dudley? Did he not guard her?"

"He is with Lane in the fields. Of a certain, Maela would not take her dog to church, though some do. Lane set Dudley upon her trail, but the dog became distraught. He has shadowed Lane since her disappearance."

"Did Maela take anything with her? Clothing? Food?"

Rachel shook her head. "Nothing that we could discover. Even her kittens are here."

It was a silly remark, but Harry did not notice at the time. It did not seem strange to believe that Maela would have taken kittens along had she been able.

Harry ate the evening meal with the Flemings. Despite his distress, he smiled to see Lane and Lottie together, evidently well matched and happy. Lottie now attended church regularly, and she spoke of Jesus as her personal Friend.

"It gives me joy to hear thee speak lovingly of the Lord, Lottie. There was a time I despaired of thee," Harry teased gently.

"Lane is patient, as is Jesus. Thy witness did break fallow ground, Harry, and Lane reaped the harvest."

"An abundant harvest," Lane added, to Harry's surprise. The tall yeoman had gained poise since the spring. His craggy face had softened, and his blue eyes twinkled.

"I feel peace concerning Maela, Harry. You shall find her. The Lord has assured me that His will shall be done, even in this trial." Lottie's round face was sober, yet calm.

Harry nodded, unable to reply. Strange, how people he had once counseled and ministered to now offered him comfort and counsel. First Sir David, and now Lottie.

"Do you need lodging this night?" Jonas inquired after a long silence.

"Nay, I dwell at my old cottage, but King Saul has need of your hospitality. I would pay for his feed, for he does eat hearty, as you will recall. On the morrow I shall ride in search of Maela. I take leave of you for the night."

Harry lay awake for many hours, staring into the thick darkness, listening to night sounds. His feather bolster smelled musty. "Where is Maela? God, I know not where to look. I am helpless."

He sighed deeply and admitted, "I had planned to rely on

mine own strengths—the power of my horse, the edge of my sword, and the depth of my love. All of my strengths are of no use, for I have no direction. You alone know the whereabouts of Your little maid, and You alone can save her from evil."

He held Maela's needlepoint pillow against his cheek. His eyes closed against the pressing darkness. "Guide me to her, Lord, if it is Thy will for me to find her. I can only lean upon Thy knowledge and strength, for mine own are as nothing."

# fourteen

*A horse is a vain hope for deliverance; despite all its great strength it cannot save. But the eyes of the Lord are on those who fear him, on those whose hope is in his unfailing love.*
Psalm 33:17-18 (NIV)

Early the next morning, Harry returned to the Fleming farm, rested and eager to set out. He had decided to begin his search at Bishop Carmichael's estate, Parminster Court, at least a half-day's ride away. The bishop was highest on his list of suspects. Exactly what he would do once he reached the ancient abbey he did not know, but he felt sure the Lord would give him wisdom at the proper time.

The sky was streaked in glorious sunrise when Harry arrived; Jonas had just emerged from the house with Dudley at his heels. Harry called out a greeting, and the dogs rushed to meet one another, tails wagging. "I would collect my horse and set out in search of Maela. I intend to begin my search at Parminster," Harry explained in passing.

But to Harry's shock, his horse was pacing in circles, sweating profusely and looking sorely distressed. "Saul, art thou ill?" The symptoms were clear: colic. Harry began to lead the groaning horse around the barnyard in wide circles. Saul frequently cocked his tail, but to no avail; he had a painful blockage. The great horse was helpless. His dark eyes looked to Harry for relief, but Harry could do nothing to help aside from keeping him on his feet and walking, hour after hour. Jonas offered to help, but Saul pinned back his ears and bared long yellow teeth. In his agony, he would allow no one but Harry to lay a hand upon him.

Harry could not be angry at the hapless horse, but he fretted inwardly. Once, when they stopped for a moment, Saul rested his enormous head upon Harry's shoulder and blew out a heavy sigh. Leaning his face against the horse's face, Harry closed his eyes and tried to be calm and accepting. *I did ask for Thy help, Lord. When am I to receive it?*

Lane had gone to town that morning. He returned at noon, riding his roan cob at a rapid clip. Dismounting, he left his horse standing and ran to Harry's side. "I bear tidings of great import, Harry! The village is rife with talk about Bishop Carmichael. He has arrived without notice, and our fellowship shall surely suffer his wrath. The Reverend Master Tompkins has informed him of the believers' activities, of Marston's involvement with Puritan leaders, and our apparent disdain for the church's liturgy. The bishop now resides at the King's Head Inn, along with a large retinue. It would appear that he has come to conquer, not to direct our manner of worship. The townsfolk are greatly disquieted."

The two men absently circled the barnyard. Saul's big head bobbed faster above Harry's shoulder as their pace increased. Lane added, "Armed men wearing Carmichael livery have visited—some say raided—nigh every freehold, husbandry, and business in the parish. They appear to search for something of value. Could it be Lord Trenton they seek? Or Maela? Would the bishop know of her existence?"

At last Harry spoke, his voice deep with repressed anxiety, "He knows, and desires her for his own. At least we may know that she is not already in his power."

"I have further news," Lane continued. "Dob Titwhistle has been sighted at the King's Head. The man is clothed in velvets and furs, and while in his cups he did boast of his connections with sacred and influential personages. There is little doubt that he is in the bishop's employ!"

"Dob!" Harry blurted, then fell silent. This alliance was unexpected; he had discounted the rumors, but now they proved true.

"I must now inform my family," Lane excused himself. Harry noticed that Dudley followed the yeoman into the house. It would appear that the young dog had transferred his loyalty.

And still, Harry could only walk his horse and pray for patience. Saul groaned in relief when the rapid pace slowed. Harry rubbed around the gelding's twitching ears. "Forgive me, my friend. I forget thy pain while dwelling upon mine own."

At last, more than two hours past noon, Saul relieved himself. Harry gave a fervent prayer of thanks, for, aside from his need of Saul, he was greatly attached to the horse. It had troubled him to see his friend in distress and be helpless to give aid.

*Lord, I apologize for my former arrogance. Thy will be done on earth as it is in heaven. Had I ridden to Parminster Court this morning, I would have missed Lane's vital information.*

Saul seemed subdued, but he was himself again. He bunted Harry affectionately with his Roman nose, pricked his ears at Ragwort, and even nibbled at the hay Harry offered. "He shall recover," Jonas diagnosed. "Back to normal in a day or two. He is of a kind that recovers quickly."

Harry rubbed Saul's soft gray nose, smiling when the horse threw his head up in annoyance. Saul disliked having his nose touched, but sometimes Harry couldn't resist. Saul's big lips flopped together noisily as he reached for the carrot Harry held just out of reach. Harry gave him the treat and hugged his warm neck.

Jonas smiled as he watched. "You two are well matched."

"How so?"

"In appearance you are like, both large and powerful beyond others of your kind, comely of face and form, and boisterous by nature, capturing the notice of all whether ye will or no. You appear bold and eager for warfare, daunting your foes, yet you are tender of heart and slow to engage in battle."

Harry tried to hide embarrassment with a joke, "And we two consume fodder beyond others of our kind!"

Jonas wryly acknowledged, "True." He reached out to pat

the gelding's neck. "I know that Saul's illness has caused thee to chafe. The Lord will have His way in this, Harry, if you allow Him to lead."

Harry nodded humbly. "I asked for God's guidance, and He leads by strange paths indeed. Jonas, will you watch over Saul? I shall walk over to the castle. I know that you have searched it, yet I must see with mine own eyes."

The dogs cruised the area around Harry as he walked toward Castle Trent, always keeping within vocal range. The castle courtyard was devoid of life. No rooks perched upon the battlements.

Harry tried the kitchen door and found it unlocked. Ragwort trotted on in, scouting for rats or cats. Harry was surprised to see kegs, baskets, and cooking utensils arranged neatly against the walls or hung upon hooks. The supply of faggots was low, but tidily stacked near the hearth. The floor tiles were cracked and stained, but clean. The last time he had seen it, this kitchen had been in total disarray.

Wiping the table with one finger, he pulled it away free of dust. He checked the scullery. The supplies were low, but fresh. A side of bacon, a barrel of coarse flour, turnips, apples, carrots—plenty to feed a maid and her captor for many a day.

Moving on into the entryway, Harry felt that he was being watched. He spun around, half expecting to find Dob upon him with a pike, but the hall was empty. Only Laitha stood beside him, her nose working overtime. A barely audible whine escaped her. "What is it, lass?" Harry whispered, but Laitha merely cocked her head toward him.

Ragwort rushed past, wuffing eagerly. Harry and Laitha followed him up winding stairs to the gallery outside Maela's old chamber. There was a splintered gap in the gallery floor; a board dangled beneath, hanging by one peg. Below, the great hall stood empty.

Harry's skin crept. He did not believe in haunting spirits, yet his incipient fear could not be denied. "Lord, I need Thy strength," he breathed aloud, "for my courage does falter!"

Tentatively, he stepped into the gallery, momentarily

expecting its floor to give way. It held, protesting with creaks that seemed deafening in the silence. Harry opened the door to Maela's bedchamber. The room was empty, the hearth cold. No skinny, dirty figure greeted him with glowing dark eyes. He swallowed hard. Laitha bumped against his leg, then again turned her head and growled.

Other rooms were just as unrewarding. The master chamber was thick with dust, its rich bedstead cold and deserted. Other chambers showed signs of decay, though they had once been rich indeed. Covered furniture resembled ghosts of odd shapes and assorted sizes in the fading light. Surprisingly, there was no evidence that the castle had been looted. Fear of Hera's curses still held the superstitious at bay.

Mounting the battlements, Harry looked across the county, awed by the view. Almost he could imagine himself a baron of old, scanning the countryside for approaching enemy armies. . . but that romantic era had passed away. Unconsciously, Harry sighed.

Suddenly Laitha bristled and snarled, facing the staircase behind them. Harry glanced around, but saw nothing. He peered down the stairs; they were empty. There was no sign of Ragwort.

Awkwardly drawing his new rapier, Harry descended the steps. The tower stairs were open, giving him a clear view down to the bottom step; while below, in the living quarters, the spiral stairwell was enclosed and dark. At each landing Harry brandished the sword, his eyes darting back and forth.

There was no further sign of Maela. Had he been mistaken? Perhaps others had straightened the kitchen since Hera Coats's death. Or. . .Harry inwardly winced. Perhaps the girl was being held in the dungeons. He had not previously considered that possibility. She might even be—

*Nay, I will not regard it.* Shaking his head, Harry hurried to the great hall. He had not yet examined it from ground level.

Loose, dry rushes rustled as he strode into the vaulted room. Its walls were hung with rusted rows of iron helmets, crossed swords, and battle-axes, trophies of an earlier day.

The head table was empty, filmed with dust. High-backed chairs lined it on one side. The lower tables were lined with crude benches. Scars of knives, swords, and axes marked their rotting wood. Harry tried to visualize the room filled with knights, lords, and fighting men of old, but the aura of decay impeded his imagination.

Laitha sniffed along one wall and began to quiver and whine. She must have found a rat hole. The hound did not usually bark and yammer about vermin—apparently the castle's eerie gloom had even affected her.

Ragwort was also barking somewhere, a shrill, frantic bark. He must have cornered a rat. Harry whistled, but he knew the dog would not respond immediately. Ragwort's barking and Laitha's whimpering exacerbated Harry's urge to leave. Approaching the fireplace, he considered using the secret passageway for a hasty exit. He wished for a torch. "Come, Laitha."

She did not come.

"Laitha! Come hither unto me," he snapped.

Reluctantly she obeyed, looking cowed, as though he had whipped her. "Ragwort!" Harry called and whistled again, waxing impatient as his desire to depart grew.

Silent drafts wafted the mildewed, tattered banners overhead. The hair on Harry's nape tingled. The castle's ghostly air of desolation had vanquished even his bold insouciance. "Forget the dog," he growled. "He can find his own way home."

Harry drew his sword again and reached for the lever. Laitha whimpered and growled. She pressed against his leg, looking nearly as confused as Harry felt. What was she trying to tell him?

He pulled the lever, and the secret door slid open.

# fifteen

*Unto thee, O Lord, do I lift up my soul. O my God,*
*I trust in thee: let me not be ashamed, let not mine enemies*
*triumph over me. Yea, let none that wait on thee be ashamed:*
*let them be ashamed which transgress without cause.*
Psalm 25:1-3

Maela sat up, feeling stiff in every joint and muscle. "Sir Hanover?" she questioned, forgetting that he was no longer a knight. Her only answer was the scuffling, squeaking fight of rats in a corner behind the casks.

It was midafternoon, she deduced by the light from her ventilation holes. Her father usually released her at night, allowing her to wash, cook, and clean, though twice she had been denied the privilege when someone came to search the keep by night. Trenton watched her vigilantly, but she had made no effort to escape. In spite of her dire situation, Maela was at peace. During her long confinement she had spent many hours in prayer, and she knew that God was at work in her circumstances.

Rising, she rolled her head and shoulders, trying to ease their stiffness, and walked the perimeter of her prison chamber. Not only had her father known about the secret tunnel, he had also known of, and used, this hidden wine cellar. He fondly believed that he alone knew of the tunnel's existence, and Maela never dreamed of telling him that she had betrayed its secret to an outsider.

Over many years, Hera Coats had drained Castle Trent's store of inferior wines and liquors; all the while, Trenton's extensive collection of superior vintages had lain safely hidden in its secret chamber. He often consoled himself thereby during his enforced exile, imbibing until his problems faded from memory.

There was a crunch, a rattle, and the door to Maela's prison slowly opened inward. Trenton entered, rushlight in hand. "Ishy, fill this jug from that keg there," he ordered, closing the door. "I wish to speak with thee."

"Of what, sir?" she asked, obediently filling the jug with a dark liquid. Some spilled to the floor before she could stop the tap.

"Wastrel!" Hanover shouted, seized the jug, and clouted her shoulder. Maela fell back against the kegs, bruising her back. She said nothing.

Her father took a long draught from the jug then gave a satisfied sigh and burp. "Ishy," he began, wiping his mouth with one stained sleeve. "Thou art a comely wench, and, as was thy mother before thee, well suited to warm a nobleman's. . . er. . .heart. I have chosen well for thee. Titus will supply thine every desire."

Had these days of selfless service been for nothing? The kindness she had lavished upon this undeserving man must have soaked into barren ground! For a moment Maela forgot to trust God and blurted, "Do you care so little for your only daughter that you would sell her as a slave?"

Trenton choked slightly and spilled brandy down his shirt-front. "Come again? Did you say 'slave'? Was thy mother a slave, chit? She did enter into my house willingly." His mocking tone faded at the last, and a pensive frown wrinkled his brow. "She was fair beyond expression, and love welled in her eyes at sight of me," he mused. "Ah, Artemis," he shook his head sadly.

"My mother did love thee ere she entered thy house. I love not the bishop. I despise the man!"

"Wherefore? Titus is considered well favored, handsome of face and figure. Ladies of the court find the fellow fascinating."

"He repels and frightens me! My heart belongs to another, a man far exceeding the bishop in every particular. In his keeping my heart shall remain until my death or his."

"A nobleman?"

"He is noble in spirit, bearing, and countenance, if not in title. His father was a Spanish exile of noble blood, his mother a yeoman's daughter."

"Indeed? You had not claimed a lover ere now, which was wiser of thee, for I shall discover the blackguard and skewer him ere dawn." He hitched his sword into a more comfortable position. "Then thy heart will be free once again. Who is it?"

"Sir Hanover. . .Father, have you no mercy in your soul? I would no more betray him to thee than. . .than I would harm thee with mine own hands! Where will this killing end but in thine own murder?"

He scoffed. "Preach at me again, will you? I weary of thy tirades. Do not the Scriptures speak ill of a nagging woman? In truth, I expect to die by the sword, as I have lived. 'Tis an honorable death. I shall be disgraced by female baggage—of high or low station—neither to hang nor to face the block! I have done nothing worthy of such a death."

" 'It is given unto man once to die, and after that the judgment.' " Maela quoted. "Take thought for thine eternal soul, my father, before thine hour is upon thee. I would not have thee go to judgment unprepared."

"You speak as the very devil!" Trenton protested. "I am a good enough man; I support the church with my tithes and give every man his due. Of late, God has cruelly removed from me all that I valued on earth. Surely, He will be merciful to me in the end."

"There can be no mercy from the Father unless we come to Him through the Son, Jesus Christ. This He has stated clearly in the Scripture. The church cannot save thee. Thy good works cannot save thee."

Trenton's eyes narrowed. "I have not heard this nonsense before. 'Tis heresy, for the queen's church alone gives absolution. You shall burn at the stake should your heresy reach less merciful ears than mine own."

"I beg of thee to listen, my father. I fear not death, for to be absent from the body is to be present with the Lord, and my

Lord is my light and my salvation. I look for His coming with longing, and fear not an eternity in His presence. I have accepted Christ's sacrifice for my sins, and have repented from my wicked ways; therefore, I need not fear God's holy wrath. It will never fall upon me, for Christ's blood has washed away my sins for all eternity."

Hanover could only stare. "You are indeed Ishmaela, the daughter of Artemis Coats? How have you learned this heresy?"

"I learned it from the Bible, and I learned it from the man I love and intend to marry."

Slowly, Trenton rose and pulled his rapier from its scabbard. He twisted it, watching the light reflect from its polished surfaces. Approaching Maela, he touched one edge of the blade to her throat. "Recant, thou recusant witch. I would as soon slay thee as see thee wed to any but a man of my choosing. You are useless to me unless you follow after my will."

Maela did not flinch. "Then slay me, sir, for I shall recant neither of my love for Jesus Christ nor of my love for Harry."

"Harry, is it? Stubborn wench." Hanover tickled her throat and collarbones with the sharp point of his weapon. "Like thy mother thou art. Thine eyes are mine, however—dark as sin. Except," he paused, "there is strength in thine eyes, and goodness. You have a stronger character by far than your mother's, and more virtuous by far than mine. I do believe you would face death with courage, Ishy, for I could easily have killed you just now, and you know it well. I have killed before. Yet, the daughter of Hanover Trenton, a commoner's wife? I cannot allow it. You would perish of labor or boredom. You were raised to court life, wench."

"You know not how I was raised, sir, for you were here but seldom. Of late, I have lived as a yeoman's daughter. I did clean, bake, sew, reap, winnow, and all other tasks the life does require, and I am the stronger for it. You have seen me labor for your comfort and ease in this castle these many days—did I appear to suffer at it? I fear not work, for God is pleased by my labors. I do all for His glory, not for mine own."

"And is thy lover worthy of thee?"

Maela was uncertain whether he mocked her, but she answered, "Harry is worthy of the highest and best in the land, sir, for a better man I cannot imagine. He is God's humble servant and the servant of all mankind. No man alive has a more generous heart. He did take into his care a dirty, bitter, hopeless child, and, expecting nothing in return, did give her freely of all he possessed. Through his love, I learned of God's love."

For a moment, she saw a flicker of human feeling cross his face. "A veritable saint, this fellow—" He paused abruptly, still pointing his sword at Maela's bare throat. His eyes lifted to the ventilation cracks. "I did hear a dog bark. Intruders storm the castle yet again." He swore softly. His eyes hardened. "Keep still, wench, or I shall slit thy throat with impunity, for my life is more to me than thine."

"Father," Maela said quietly as he headed for the door.

He stopped and turned slowly. When his eyes met hers, she saw in them a new expression, a softening. "What, Ishy?"

"Thou art my father, and I do honor thee greatly."

For a long moment he showed no reaction. Then he strained as though attempting to swallow with a dry throat. At last he simply turned and slipped silently through the doorway.

As the door swung shut, Maela stopped it short. This time her father was too absorbed in listening for sounds of the intruder to notice that the latch did not click.

She heard the tunnel door open and close at the far end. Venturing into the narrow passageway, she felt her way along the wall. The light from outside was dim. She could see little.

A snuffling sound from above startled her. Peering at the wall to her right, she saw a long crack near the ceiling with a series of foot and hand holds beneath it—a peephole. She immediately climbed up. That sound had not come from a rat.

Her assumption proved correct: a dog's black nose sniffed at the crack. It pulled away for a moment, and Maela dimly caught sight of a patched face and empty eye sockets.

"Laitha," she dared to breathe. The dog began to tremble and whimper happily, but she could not understand Maela's position within the thick wall. "Tell Harry where I am," Maela choked. The knowledge that Harry must be near almost reduced her to tears.

Laitha disappeared from Maela's sight. For a minute more the girl waited, then lowered herself with a hand on the far wall. Did she dare try to escape? Where was Trenton? At the end of the passage Maela descended the few stairs to the wooden door, but she could not open it. Its latch must be on the outside. She hurried back to the rock ladder and scrambled up, bracing herself with one foot upon the outside wall.

She caught a glimpse of Laitha across the great room and heard what sounded like a man's voice. Was it Harry? Dared she take the chance that it was? Should she be mistaken, her father would most likely kill her and leave her body forever undiscovered within the castle walls. But if it were Harry and she said nothing, she could lose her only chance!

Suddenly she heard strange sounds, a clash as of metal upon metal, and men's voices shouting. She could not understand the words, but thought she recognized Harry's voice. "Harry! Harry, I am here!" she shouted. Her voice was lost in the clatter.

As soon as the panel had slid open, Harry had known he was in for trouble. Laitha had tried to warn him, so he was hardly surprised when Hanover Trenton leaped through the opening, thrusting a sword at Harry's head. He barely had time to fall away before the older man was upon him again.

Harry lifted his sword to parry the thrust, finding it difficult to maneuver while seated upon the floor. Laitha helped him by getting in the way. When Trenton tripped over her cringing form, Harry seized his chance and crawled beneath the head table, between chair legs, and out the other side. The disgruntled nobleman shouted curses, but he did not harm the dog. Laitha yelped and scuttled blindly into the tunnel, seeking peace and shelter.

"Come hither and fight, coward!" Hanover Trenton shouted. "Thou blackguard! How did you know of the passage? What evil arts revealed it unto thee?"

"No evil art, Lord Trenton, but thine own flesh did reveal it. Ishmaela told me of the tunnel. Where is she?" Harry asked from the other side of the table. He was now upon his feet and had his cloak wrapped around his left arm as a kind of shield.

Their voices echoed from stone walls and ceilings. Hanging banners rustled like whispering voices of long ago. The setting sun, released by a passing cloud, suddenly poured light through the hall's cross-shaped windows. Brilliant golden crosses appeared across the walls and floor, one spotlighting Trenton. Harry saw fatigue and strain in his opponent's lined face.

Hanover stepped out of the light. "Let me conjecture—thou art the esteemed Harry, the man my foolish daughter professes to love more than life itself." As he spoke, he casually reached into the fireplace and pulled the lever to close his secret tunnel. He would not allow Harry to escape by that means.

Harry's eyes flickered, but he did not lose his guard. "I am Harry the joiner. I was privileged to tutor Maela through her childhood, and have become her mentor and friend."

"Then you love not the wench?"

Before Harry could reply, Hanover leaped atop the table and fell upon him with a flashing sword. Far from comfortable with his narrow rapier, Harry did well to parry the varied thrusts of his enemy, let alone launch any form of attack.

One vicious encounter breached his guard; with lightning speed, Trenton's rapier slashed down upon Harry's left shoulder. Harry dodged, but he was not quick enough; the sword sliced into the muscle of his upper arm. He made no sound, though his face whitened and sweat beaded his forehead. His sleeve darkened rapidly, feeling hot and damp against his skin.

Another cloud obscured the sun. Once again, the hall fell into grim shadow.

Trenton stepped back to catch his breath. "Ishmaela is pledged to Bishop Carmichael. In the abbey, she shall be treated as a veritable queen, wanting nothing. What life would she have with such as thee? A hovel in the countryside or a hovel in the village, twenty children, and never enough to eat. The daughter of Hanover Trenton deserves better than thy dirty hands upon her, joiner man. Come and let me slice those cursed hands from thy limbs!"

Harry's teeth clenched against the pain and fury. Should this. . .this scoundrel kill him, Maela's doom was sealed. Would he, could he, allow himself to be cut to ribbons in this way? He would not.

*God, I ask Thine immediate aid! The situation is dire, indeed.*

Letting go of his injured arm, he walked boldly toward Sir Hanover. Sweat dripped from his nose, but he gave it no heed. The sun broke through, again flaming cross signs throughout the hall. Harry's upraised sword caught a ray that turned it into fire.

"You think not to—" Sir Hanover began, then Harry was upon him. Pounding and battering, he made the smaller man use his sword as a shield against the attack, giving him no time to set himself for fencing thrusts or lunges.

The tables were turned—for as long as Harry's rapier did not break. Ignoring his wound, Harry used his superior strength to advantage. Trenton was soon bleeding from several nicks and cuts; his breath wheezed from his lungs.

"Slay me quick," he panted, staggering back from another of Harry's assaults. "I beg of thee, turn me not over to the queen, but slay me like the man of honor I have ever been!"

Harry stopped abruptly. Echoes of clashing swords still rang among the rafters. "I would slay thee not, sir!" He sounded astonished at the very idea. He stood with his back to the entryway, his chest heaving. Hanover Trenton drooped against a table, gasping for breath.

A voice bellowed, "Nay? But I would!"

The shout was followed by a swish-thump, and Hanover staggered back with an arrow in his left biceps. His agonized cry rang in Harry's ears.

Both men stared wildly about, then heard a laugh from above. Dob Titwhistle stood upon the high gallery, longbow in hand. "The next shall pierce thy wicked heart. Long I have dreamed of the moment when our fortunes would reverse, Hanover Trenton—the knight that was! And thou, joiner—a sorcerer, indeed! I would give thee trade—the baseborn wench in return for this! It did bite me upon the leg, and deserves not to live." He pulled Ragwort from a sack and suspended him by the scruff of the neck. "Work your sorcery now, if you can!"

He drew back his arm and tossed the wailing dog lightly into the air. Before Harry's horrified eyes, his beloved pet spun, legs outspread, high above, then hurtled downward. Without conscious thought, Harry dashed across the room, hurdling tables and benches. His rapier clattered to the floor. With his one good arm outstretched, he flung himself face first and caught Ragwort only inches from the stone floor. He skidded along the floor on his belly and stopped just before the fireplace.

Dob had leaned against the gallery railing to watch Ragwort's flight, but the rotted wood could not bear his weight. With a grinding crash it gave way, and Dob plummeted, screaming, headfirst into the floor. The fate he had wished upon a dog came to him instead. Boards and splinters continued to rain upon his body in the dreadful silence that followed.

The last gleam of sunlight disappeared, casting the hall into shadow once again. Harry watched as Trenton, with clenched teeth and a deep groan, drew the arrow from his own arm and threw it down. One-handed, he wrapped a handkerchief around the wound.

Then Trenton limped across the room and squatted beside his former retainer's body. A table blocked Harry's view, but he heard a satisfied grunt. "I take only what you did owe, traitor." Trenton rose, still stuffing something inside his jerkin, staggered to a table, pulled out the bench, and sat down, exhausted.

Harry scooted up to lean his head and shoulders against the wall and cuddled his trembling dog. Ragwort seemed to be in shock; he clung to Harry's neck like a baby to its mother.

"I have no longer any war with thee, Harry the joiner. Thou art, indeed, a noble man. Take the wench and Godspeed." Trenton's voice was tired, but relieved. Retrieving his fallen sword, he made as though to sheathe it, but at that moment there was a rush and clatter in the doorway, and several men-at-arms entered the room and lined the wall on either side of the door. Each held a lighted torch and a crossbow.

Bishop Carmichael followed his men into the room. His dark eyes quickly assessed the situation, showing some surprise at Dob's violent death. "I see that my faithful dunce has met an untimely end. 'Tis fitting, no doubt, that one of so little wit should unwittingly cause his own demise."

The bishop cut a dashing figure, clad in black from head to toe: velvet hat with a long aigrette plume, slashed doublet and trunk hose showing gold satin lining, muscular legs in tight netherhose, jeweled buckles upon his shoes, and a satin cloak with velvet lining flung over his shoulders. His black goatee was neatly trimmed; heavy hair curled above his starched collar. A handsome appearance he made, but no beauty marked his expression. He approached Trenton, but eyed Harry. "Introduce thy recumbent companion, I pray thee, Hanover."

"Bishop Carmichael, may I present Harry the joiner, lately employed by Marston, as I recall. I have long expected thee, Titus. The sight of thy face brings me pleasure." Trenton rose to greet his friend and bowed politely.

The bishop smiled slightly but did not return the courtesy. "Thy pleasure shall doubtless be short-lived, but let us enjoy it while we may. And this Harry the joiner is. . . ? A relation of thine, perhaps?"

"Nay. He prowled about my castle, and I did apprehend him here."

"Indeed." The bishop appeared to dismiss Harry as inconsequential. "Let us not linger here to no purpose. Hanover, where is the wench? I have come for her, you perceive, though I never imagined myself so fortunate as to find thee here as well. For too many days I have endured the propinquity of that," he waved a lazy hand at Dob's corpse, "in order to locate the wench. Almost I discarded this repugnant accomplice, but here, at last, my Christian forbearance has been remunerated in full. The odious Dob did serve me well ere he departed to his reward."

Trenton stared blankly. "I comprehend thee not. You have come for Ishmaela?"

"Of a certain. Tales of her exquisite pulchritude reached even unto Parminster Court, and I did deduce thereby that my protracted wait need quickly end. I would have her, sir. Kindly divulge her location." A salacious grin showed every tooth in the bishop's head, but his black eyes were like death.

"I regret the trouble you have endured, Titus; and all for nothing, for my daughter has—"

The bishop interrupted dryly. "I receive ample reparation for my trouble. I shall delight in the wench's abundant charms at my leisure, but equally gratifying will be the spectacle of thy head upon the White Tower wall. I shall behold thy rotting carcass in a gibbet yet!"

Harry watched Hanover's jaw drop and felt pity for the friendless man whose entire world had crashed into ruin. He quoted for all to hear, " 'None that wait on the Lord shall be ashamed: they will be ashamed which transgress without cause.' Place thy hope and trust in God, sir. He alone is always faithful, just, and merciful."

Trenton heard him and turned. For an instant his eyes met Harry's; then, before the men-at-arms could react, he lunged straight at Carmichael with sword outthrust. In the blink of an eye, the bishop was impaled upon the rapier's point.

"Be merciful to me, Jesus Christ!" Hanover shouted. Leaving his sword, he fled through the door. Chaos and confusion ensued—some men stopping to load their crossbows, others bounding in pursuit of the knight, a few gaping in horror at their fallen leader. Two rushed to tend the bishop, but there was nothing to be done. Trenton's blade had pierced his heart.

While their attention was diverted, Harry scrambled to his feet, reached into the fireplace, quietly pulled the lever, stepped into the passageway, and closed the panel. He was surprised to find that the tunnel was not entirely dark. Trenton had left a rushlamp upon the floor. It still shone brightly, though the rush was burning short.

Harry picked it up. "Maela?" He spoke softly lest the men in the great hall hear him.

A low "woof" was the only reply. Harry followed the sound to find Laitha waiting before the tunnel's side door. Ragwort struggled weakly, and Harry set him down. The terrier limped over to Laitha and cowered against her. She licked his muzzle, sensing his fear.

"Is Maela in there?" Harry asked. He pressed the latch and pushed at the door. It groaned in protest, but gradually gave way. Harry's head began to swim. The wound in his shoulder had drained his strength. His sleeve was blood soaked and stiffening. He placed his right hand over the cut to stem the blood flow and, putting his good shoulder to the heavy door, soon gained entrance to another tunnel. A set of very narrow steps led steeply upward. "Maela?" he said again.

"Harry!" Footsteps descended the stairs, and Maela threw herself into his arms.

## sixteen

*The Lord God said, "It is not good for the man to be alone.
I will make a helper suitable for him."*
Genesis 2:18 (NIV)

She was trembling, sobbing for joy. Harry kissed her hair and
held her close with one arm, marveling at her sweetness after
so many days of bondage. Her very spirit seemed to glow
from within, and her hair smelled delightful. The dogs whimpered and danced about them. Maela's appearance had done
wonders for Ragwort's morale.

"We dare not tarry here," Harry warned. He wanted to
sound loving, but his lips and tongue felt wooden.

Maela lifted her face from his shirtfront and nodded in
agreement. "Let us hurry. My father may return at any
moment."

"I think he shall not return," Harry said slowly. His voice
sounded mushy. "I think he is dead."

"You killed him?" Maela wailed. "Alas, but I had only just
told him of Jesus and the cleansing blood! And now you have
shed his blood?"

"Nay," Harry managed to tell her. "I slew him not. I—" He
staggered back, unable to support Maela's extra weight.

Maela gripped his arms, and her right hand came away red
with blood. In startled understanding, she took the rushlight
from his weak grasp. "Sit thee down."

Harry almost collapsed upon the sandy tunnel floor.

"Harry! Oh, my beloved, do not die! I will not have it, do
you hear me?" She pressed her ear to his chest. His heartbeat
was steady, but it was not strong. Examining his wound, she
found that it still bled. She began to rip up one of her petticoats

to provide a bandage. Once the wound had been bound, she felt better.

"Come, my Harry. We must hurry to Rachel. She is skilled at healing."

Blindly, he staggered after her. At the outside entrance to the tunnel, she climbed up to check the surroundings then dropped back down. "Night has fallen, and no enemy is in sight. Climb out, and I shall push thee from behind."

Harry obeyed without question. He crawled a few feet away from the tunnel and flopped belly down.

Maela crawled to his side and checked his shoulder. The wound had bled again; her petticoat strips were soaked through. She tore off more strips and wrapped them around the others. Ragwort supervised her every move; his cold, wet nose was everywhere her hands needed to be. He was not about to let Harry out of his sight again that day. Laitha lay between Harry's outstretched legs.

The night was cool, and Harry shivered. He could travel no farther. Maela moved to his uninjured side, leaned against a tree, and pulled him into her arms as well as she could. His cheek rested upon her bosom. She felt his heart racing weakly.

"Maela?" he croaked, surprising her. She had thought him unconscious.

"I am here," she soothed, pressing her lips to his hair. "Conserve thy strength, Harry, my beloved one, and pray. God will send aid, I doubt not."

He snuggled closer and heaved a sigh. "Leave me not," he begged.

"Never shall I leave thee of mine own accord, Harry."

"I never wished to leave thee. I was obliged. . ." his voice trailed away.

It was cloudy, but no rain had fallen that day. Nevertheless, dampness seeped through Maela's cloak and chilled her to the bone. She worried that Harry would survive his injury only to die of exposure. He was asleep, breathing roughly through his mouth.

Absorbed in thought, she almost missed Laitha's low growl

of warning. Ever vigilant, the greyhound pointed her long nose away from the castle, into the woods. Ragwort lifted his head from Harry's chest and whimpered. Suddenly, a large shape barreled into them, and Maela was swarmed by a licking, whining, wagging, bristly hound. "Dudley!"

"Maela?" A quiet voice spoke from the darkness.

"Lane, we are here," she answered in the same guarded tone. "Harry is injured."

Lane and Jonas appeared at her side and knelt to examine the unconscious man. "We must make haste," Jonas said. "He is poorly." They lifted Harry between them and carried him off, moving quietly. Maela ran to keep up.

"The woods are filled with armed men, searching." Lane gave her a quick glance and added, "Welcome home, Maela. We did greatly miss thee."

Rachel washed her hands with soap and took a sharp needle out of a bowl of strong spirits to thread it with gut. Lane and Jonas lifted Harry upon the table, and Rachel set to work. Lottie had promised to pray in another room, for she could not bear to watch. Maela's job was holding Harry's head still. The men held his legs and arms. He had unfortunately regained consciousness.

Rachel unwrapped the wound, which immediately started bleeding again. She pried open the slice and poured alcohol inside upon the raw flesh. Harry let out a shout that nearly lifted the thatching overhead, then clenched his teeth, determined not to cry out again.

The razor-sharp rapier had made a three-inch slice down the meaty outer portion of Harry's upper arm. Instead of stitching a mere cut, Rachel had to hold the slice in place and sew around it. Even if the wound healed well, the muscle would never be quite as strong as before.

While Rachel stitched, Harry looked up into Maela's eyes. Instead of observing the surgery as she had planned, Maela returned Harry's upside-down gaze. She knew he needed her as a kind of anchor in the storm. Her thumbs caressed his stubbled cheeks.

"I approve thy neat beard," she told him. "Thou art a goodly man, indeed."

He closed his eyes, then looked up at her again. "Thou. . . art well?" he gasped as Rachel made another stitch.

"Well enough. It was cold in that chamber, but I had sufficient food and water. Sir Hanover allowed me freedom within the castle each night. He was not unkind."

"I thank God," Harry whispered. His face looked almost green. It frightened Maela. She laid her cheek against Harry's forehead, feeling the chill of his flesh. "Lane, he needs a blanket. He will not kick while you are away, I am sure. Find a blanket for him, I beg of thee!" Lane obediently found some blankets and helped Maela cover Harry's shivering body with them.

Jonas had been quiet throughout the ordeal, his eyes closed in silent prayer. When Rachel at last stepped back, Jonas breathed, "Amen."

The shoulder was neatly bound with clean cloths, and this time very little blood seeped through. Harry was given a drink, then placed before the fire to rest and warm up while the others ate a late supper. Laitha pressed close to Harry's side, seeming to understand that he was injured. Ragwort sat beside Maela at the table, shamelessly begging for scraps. Though Dudley seemed happy to have Maela back, he lay at Lane's feet.

Harry slipped into a restless slumber.

Bright sunlight streamed through the open doorway and disturbed Harry's sleep. Blinking painfully, he lifted his hand to block the glare.

"Harry, thou art awake!" Maela hurried to his side and bent over his pallet. His blanket had slipped when he moved his arm; she tucked it back around his chest.

"More or less so," he admitted. "It is morning?"

"Nay, 'tis past nooning. You have slept the day away." She settled beside him on the floor, her kirtle and petticoats fluffing out around her. "Do you hunger or thirst?"

"Yea, for sight of thee," he smiled weakly. "Thou art a sight for sore eyes, and mine are, of a certain, sore." His gaze traveled from her face down to her mound of skirts, then back up again. Her waistcoat was modestly straight-laced, but the curves beneath it could not be concealed. "You have changed greatly, my little one. Thou art a child no longer."

Her face colored rosily. "I had hoped you would notice."

"Tush! It could scarcely be helped," he remarked dryly. "I am not a blind man."

Rachel walked in. "Ah, I see that our Harry has awakened! Does thy shoulder pain thee, lad?" She took Maela's place and began to unwrap the bandages. Maela hovered near his head, just out of sight.

"It pains me little. I would rise and eat, Rachel."

She regarded him with pursed lips. "Thy color has improved, and there is no fever as I had feared. You may rise, if you wish to. Maela, fetch me Lane's shirt from the line. Harry's shirt is stained and rent."

After replacing his bandages, Rachel helped him pull a clean shirt over his head and slip his good arm into the sleeve. The other arm was bound against his body.

"I fear for Lane's second-best shirt," Rachel shook her head. "You have greater breadth of shoulder. Make no sudden moves."

"I have not the capacity for sudden movement." Slowly, giving his spinning head time to clear, Harry sat up, then drew his legs under him and rose. All went dark, so he simply stood still, waiting for his vision to clear. Slowly, awkwardly, he tucked the shirt into his woolen hose. A jerkin could wait; for now he was at least decently clad.

He blinked at Rachel. "I hunger."

"I might have known," she chuckled. "There is provender aplenty. Cold mutton, cheese, apples, and bread baked fresh this morning."

Harry tucked in with a will and felt much stronger once his belly had been filled and his thirst slaked. His shoulder throbbed, but he could ignore it. Despite her protests, he helped Rachel clear away the mess from his meal.

"Where has Maela gone?" he wondered.

Rachel answered calmly, "Lottie did require her aid at the laundry."

Slowly, carefully, Harry walked toward the pond where the two women bent to their task, pounding soggy garments upon rocks and rough boards. Harry could hear them talking together, ". . .and whatever shall I do without thy company, Maela? I do love Rachel, but she is not the friend to me thou art."

"The Lord shall supply thee friendships aplenty, Lottie, dear sister. Women of our age are abundant in the fellowship. And, of a certain, Lane shall be thy dearest friend, as Harry is mine." Maela dunked Harry's shirt into a bucket of clean water. The extensive bloodstain had faded into a dull yellow patch.

"I do love Lane, but our conversation is limited. He speaks of field production, labor ills, and the imminent foaling of a favorite mare. I speak of village gossip and the furnishings of our home. 'Tis a sad—Oh, Harry! I heard not thine approach!"

"Harry!" Maela sat back on her heels, shaking icy, reddened hands. "You should be abed! Does Rachel know of thine escape?" She jumped up and caught hold of his arm.

He nodded. "She knows I could remain abed no longer. I am on the mend and would have private speech with thee."

Maela's eyes widened at his serious tone. She glanced at Lottie, then nodded. "In the barn out of this wind, perhaps?"

Harry let her help him to the barn. Inside, they sat upon a bench and leaned against the wall. Two kittens scampered over to greet Maela. She picked up the calico kitten; the golden tiger kitten playfully attacked her skirts. "There were four kittens when I left, but Lane says the tom killed two. I don't understand why." She snuggled a kitten against her face. "They are so innocent and dear."

"Though Ragwort has sworn off kittens, I do not believe we can take them with us," Harry said slowly. " 'Twill be difficult enough to travel without them."

"Travel?" Maela's chin jerked up. Her dark eyes bored into

Harry. "Thou art not—" Then one word sank in. "We?"

He looked surprised. "We travel to Lincoln as soon as we are wed. My family does expect us ere Christmastide."

Maela looked dazed. "Wed? I heard nothing about a wedding." She released the kitten to join its sister.

Now Harry looked puzzled. " 'Twas understood that we would wed except for thy father's objection. Now that is withdrawn, and we are free to marry."

"My father. . .is not dead, so far as we know, Harry. He has eluded capture."

"Praise be to God!" Harry exclaimed, his face lighting up.

Maela was confused. "Thou art glad of this news? He can no longer sell me to the bishop, who is dead, but he is unlikely to approve our—"

"Thy father gave me his blessing ere the bishop appeared last night," Harry announced.

"He did? I cannot conceive of it!"

"Nevertheless, it is true. I have thy father's blessing; now I need only thy consent." Harry was beginning to wonder. Maela did not seem particularly overjoyed. "Will you become my wife, Maela? Or has thine ardor cooled during mine absence?"

She looked into his worried eyes and smiled. "I merely buried it in ashes until thy return. It retains its heat, foolish man. As though such love as mine could cool!"

"It is well, for I could not do without thee. Only anticipation of return has enabled me to bear our parting. I doubt not that my sisters shall regale thee at length with tales of my distraction." Harry smiled sheepishly and picked up Maela's hand. Their fingers twined together, and each of them felt unaccountably shy.

"Uh. . .when shall we wed?" Harry blurted. He could hardly keep his eyes from her, but feared she would find his dazzled observation rude. It was difficult to equate his beloved little tree-climbing monkey Maela with the exquisite creature at his side.

Maela immediately shifted on the bench to face him. "As soon as thou art mended; we must arrange affairs with the vicar immediately. I would not have a great festival; the simple ceremony would please me more. I shall wear my mother's finest silk gown. It is green like the corn in spring and patterned with leaves and flowers. I can fill my mother's gowns now," she boasted.

Harry did not understand the significance of this accomplishment. "Indeed?"

"And Lottie shall design my hood. She is gifted in this way."

Harry nodded, watching each animated expression light her face.

"I suppose we must have cake to distribute. Rachel baked Lottie's cake, and it looked well, though I never tasted it."

While Maela chattered on about wedding details, Harry stroked her cheek with one fingertip. It was as soft and smooth as it appeared. The finger trailed down to trace her rosy lips. At last Maela stopped talking.

"Harry," she reached up to hold his hand and pressed a kiss into his rough palm. "Thou art. . .most distracting." Delight and irritation blended in her voice. She met his gaze and stopped, inhaling sharply.

Harry kissed her parted lips and ended all discussion of wedding plans for the time being.

# seventeen

*How delightful is your love, my sister, my bride!*
*How much more pleasing is your love than wine,*
*and the fragrance of your perfume than any spice.*
Song of Songs 4:10 (NIV)

Harold Jameson and Ishmaela Andromeda Trenton exchanged vows December 3, 1567, at the Trenton parish church. The Reverend Master Cecil Tompkins performed the ceremony, and Sir David Marston, at his own insistence, gave away the bride. Lottie and Lane stood as witnesses.

The young couple honeymooned in the coppice cottage for six days. They wavered between wishing to be alone together and wanting to share these last few days with their friends. The Flemings and Sir David wisely left them alone to work out the dilemma together. They ended up spending afternoons in the company of friends, but usually returned home before the evening meal.

Maela was both thrilled and frightened by the prospect of their imminent journey. "I cannot imagine what it shall be like. Never have I left the vicinity of Castle Trent in my sixteen years. Shall we sleep beneath the stars, Harry?" She tipped her head back to look into her husband's face.

Harry stroked the silken hair that draped across his lap. They sat before the fire, as of old, but now Maela rested her head upon her husband's thigh and Laitha snuggled against her side. Ragwort, displaced, curled up on Maela's belly.

Harry shook his head, pursing his lips thoughtfully. "Nay, we must find shelter each night. We shall be several days upon the road, for I would not exhaust thee with a hard pace. We dare not give opportunity to highwaymen, Maela.

Much of our way lies through thinly settled country, rife with brigands."

"I fear not, for few would accost such a man as my husband." She reached up to caress his chest and shoulders, carefully avoiding his still-tender arm. "We have little of value to tempt a thief. Did I not hear thee say that thy savings was safe at thy home?"

"Verily, after purchasing thy steed, I have left only sufficient coins for our board and lodging; but the horses, our provisions, and you would prove ample temptation for many a villain."

Maela digested this information in silence. Changing the subject, she blurted, "And we cannot take Samson or Genevieve? I understand the necessity of leaving the poultry, but the beasts are. . .are like family to me, Harry!"

Harry sighed. They had already discussed this problem more than once. "Be thankful that Pegasus shall join us, Maela. Samson is too old for such a journey, and Genevieve would delay our travel. I have goats and sheep aplenty for thee at thy new home, my love. The Flemings promise our beasts good care and kindness all their days. We cannot ask more than this."

"I have given Dudley to Lane," she said quietly. "He shall be happier here, for his heart is Lane's as it was never mine."

"You have Laitha and Ragwort to love."

She nodded. "I regret that I trouble thee over the beasts, Harry, but I love them all so. . ." Her voice caught. "I must leave my kittens as well, and at times my heart aches. . ."

Her little sob tore at Harry's soft heart. "I would transport them all for thee, if it were possible."

"I know it well, Harry. Thou art exceedingly good to me." Brushing away her tears, she climbed into her husband's lap and snuggled close. "Truly, I need none but thee to love, Harry. I shall be content and complain no more."

Maela's new cob, a chestnut gelding called Abner, cheered her considerably. She vacillated between excitement about her new horse and feelings of regret. "Pegasus will think me fickle," she mourned, scratching her pony's furry neck. "I have never ridden another horse in his presence."

"He shall adjust to it." Harry chuckled at her nonsense. He was loading the pony's pack, testing its balance and adjusting the contents accordingly. "He receives enough attention to make thy husband sore jealous."

"Tush!" Maela slipped her arms around her husband's waist and squeezed gently. "Demanding, thou art."

Harry abandoned his work to kiss her. Lost in their own world, the young couple did not hear company approaching until George cleared his throat. They sprang apart, flushed and embarrassed.

"I beg your pardon." George grinned. "Lord Marston requests thine attendance upon him this day, Harry. It seems urgent." The stocky field hand had recently married Dovie after a somewhat rocky courtship. He seemed content with his lot, but Harry did not envy him such a contentious, conniving wife.

Harry cast a regretful glance at his wife, but obligingly accompanied George to the manor house. He left the dogs with Maela for protection.

Harry returned a few hours later and resumed his packing and preparations. Maela thought he seemed somewhat distracted. "Harry, what said his lordship?"

He glanced up, startled. "Sir David? He. . .uh. . .wished us a safe and pleasant journey." Quickly he delved into a new subject. "Have you considered that we have no ladies' saddle for thee, Maela? And I have not the funds to purchase one."

She brushed this aside. "It is of no moment. I have ridden astride since my childhood and see no reason for change."

Harry looked uncertain. " 'Twill be a long and tedious journey, and a lady rides not astride, Maela."

"Then 'tis fortunate that I am no lady, as I have told thee before. I shall wear my drawers and a full-skirted gown, and none shall know that I ride astride until I dismount. I care not what people may think as long as I shame thee not."

"You could never shame me. Maela, thou art the very light

of mine eyes!" Once again the work fell neglected as Harry fervently embraced his wife. This time the honeymooners were not interrupted.

At last, the day of departure arrived. A small crowd clustered in the Fleming barnyard to wish the travelers Godspeed. Maela felt confused—uncertain whether to laugh for joy or cry in sorrow. For so long she had dreamed of seeing new sights and meeting new people, but now that she was leaving her hometown, possibly forever, she felt bereft. Familiar faces had become extremely dear: Jonas and Rachel, Lane and Lottie, her girlfriends at church. And the knowledge that she would never again see the familiar battlements of Castle Trent keep against the horizon brought tears springing to her eyes. She allowed Harry to lift her to Abner's back, but her shoulders slumped as she adjusted her reins.

"Farewell, my dearest maiden," Rachel held her foot and kissed her hem. "I shall pray for thee daily." Tears streaked Rachel's plump face, and her chins quivered.

Maela nodded, unable to speak. Jonas held Abner's bridle. He winked and smiled at Maela, but she spotted tears in his bright eyes.

Lottie was sobbing, clinging to Lane as they approached Abner. Lane reached up to take Maela's hand. "Lottie desires me to tell thee of her undying love and gratitude. We shall miss thee greatly, Maela child."

Maela and Lottie had already exchanged several weepy good-bye hugs. Maela smiled through her own tears at Lottie's dramatics. "And I you."

Sir David himself had ridden over to bid Harry farewell. The two men had been speaking in low tones while the Flemings clustered around Maela, but now Harry reined Saul up beside his wife's mount. "We must away."

Maela was ready. Side by side they trotted down the lane and into the road. Pegasus followed on a lead rein, and the dogs loped along behind. Maela turned to wave one last time.

It was not until that afternoon, when they had passed through Bury St. Edmunds and headed toward Newmarket, that Maela noticed Harry's unease. "Wherefore do you look back so often, Harry? Are we being followed?"

He glanced over at her, his expression unreadable. "Perhaps."

A twinge of fear pinched Maela's heart. She began to pray again for God's protection, and for a while she distracted herself from the pain in her backside. Maela was unused to spending hours in a saddle, and she felt blisters forming on her inner thighs. Abner's saddle was poorly finished, and its rough edges abraded Maela's soft skin. Harry had insisted that she wear high boots to protect her lower legs, and now she was grateful to him.

She glanced back. The rolling, forested terrain concealed any possible pursuers. She sighed, thinking that travel was not as exciting and wonderful as she had dreamed.

Maela was exhausted by the time they stopped for the night at an inn on the outskirts of Newmarket. She waited in the saddle while Harry arranged lodging for the horses, and nearly fell into his arms. He half carried her into the inn and up to their room. She was unaware of anything going on around her.

Later she awoke to total darkness. Laughter and singing rose from the pub beneath the floor, and the room smelled strongly of ale and unwashed bodies. Maela sat up gingerly, very much aware of her aching legs and bottom. She felt for the blisters and was surprised to discover that they had been salved and bandaged. Dear, considerate Harry!

Laitha and Ragwort lay across the foot of the bed. Ragwort rose and staggered across the blankets to snuggle into Maela's arms. "Where is Harry?" she asked the dogs. Exhausted, Laitha only snored on. Ragwort sighed, but made no answer. Maela considered rising to search for Harry, but that would involve too much effort. Surely he would return in good time. She lay back down and quickly dozed off.

It was still dark when she awakened to Harry's kisses. Feeling warm and loved, she began to return his caresses, but he pulled away. "It pains me to wake thee, but we must away, my dearest." He was already dressed and ready, to her dismay. "The horses await us outside. I left thee to sleep until the last possible moment. We shall break our fast in the saddle."

Maela used the washbasin and chamber pot, shivering in the icy winter air. Quickly, she donned her waistcoat and full kirtle, drawers, hose, and boots. Harry helped her brush her hair, then watched as she braided it and bound it upon her head. Tying the strings of her cap, she announced, "Let us be off!"

To Maela's delighted surprise, Abner's saddle was now padded. Somewhere, Harry had found a feather pillow and fastened it upon the hard seat. "Harry," she began, but could not think of adequate praise. She simply gave him a quick hug and allowed him to boost her up.

For the next two days they kept the same schedule, stopping at convenient towns for their meals and lodging. The horses appreciated the leisurely pace and were full of life each morning. Not even little Pegasus seemed tired, though his pack was heavy. Harry had packed it carefully, evenly distributing its weight. Ragwort generally walked in the morning and rode with Harry after dinner. Laitha trotted easily beside the horses. Maela's blisters still pained her, but they did not grow worse.

They lodged on the third night in Stamford. Maela was excited when Harry told her that they were entering Lincolnshire. Another day of travel and they would be near home.

"Queen Elizabeth's minister, William Cecil, has a manor near here. Thy father has frequently sojourned there. He is well acquainted with Cecil, though not on the friendliest of terms."

"How do you know this?" Maela asked, her eyes narrowing.

The Jamesons were dining in a pleasant inn alongside the Welland River. The proprietor had gifted Laitha and Ragwort each with a knucklebone, and the dogs were pleasantly occupied thereby beneath the table.

Maela watched Harry's face redden. "He must have mentioned it to me."

"I was unaware that you had spoken with him on a casual basis."

Harry made work of chewing his tender beefsteak. He could not meet Maela's eyes. After a moment he sat back and sighed. "I cannot deceive thee longer. Thy father follows us to Lincolnshire. I have met with him each night while you did slumber."

Maela sat like stone. "How long have you known?"

"Since Sir David told me, before we did leave Trenton. I was sworn to secrecy ere I knew what I was about; I would ne'er be party to deceit otherwise. Thy father wishes to take ship at Boston harbor, where no troops shall lie in wait for him. Marston gave him a letter of introduction to a merchant there who will provide safe passage to the continent."

"He said he needed funds from the bishop to pay his passage. This was why he held me captive."

"No longer. He acquired Dob's purse, filled with Trenton rent money. It was his own by right, and full sufficient for his need. This is why he gave me his blessing, Maela. He does care for thee, in his way, and planned to sell thee only to provide for his exigency."

She grimaced. "Had he truly loved me, he would have found another way to resolve his dilemma. The bishop was a nefarious man, and my father knew it well. Love seeks not her own and places the loved one's needs first."

Harry gave her a long, sober look. "Thy father had not the Spirit within to teach him such love. 'Love bears all things, believes all things, hopes all things, and endures all things.' Have you demonstrated such love to him?"

Maela's face puckered, and tears trickled down her cheeks. She pushed her plate away. "I did try, Harry. You know not what I did endure. . ." She covered her face with both hands and sobbed.

Harry wiped his face with the tablecloth, and rose. Lifting his wife by the shoulders, he led her to their room. Laitha followed, carrying her bone, but Ragwort could not lift his. He remained under the table, gnawing frantically.

Maela slept little that night. Ragwort awakened her by scratching at the door—he had finally finished with his bone. Harry was missing again. Maela lay in bed, alone but for the dogs, staring fixedly at the low ceiling.

"Lord, I desire to love my father, though he has cast my love back into my face countless times. I know that You did instruct us to forgive seventy times seven, but I fear I have surpassed that amount already! Jesus, You have promised me love and forgiveness despite my willful ways; help me now, in the same manner, to forgive my father and truly forget his sins against me. I did not know how hard was my heart, until now."

At last, when Harry slept beside her, she snuggled against his warm side and slept peacefully.

# eighteen

*My little children, let us not love in word,*
*neither in tongue;*
*but in deed and in truth.*
1 John 3:18

Maela remounted after a rest stop, groaning as her tired backside hit the padded saddle. Abner pawed restlessly and shook his head, anticipating her command. Harry, Saul, and Pegasus waited at the roadside.

"Better?" Harry asked solicitously.

"Verily, I thank thee. Thou art indeed good to—" She stopped, staring at Laitha. Whimpering, the hound trotted ahead along the road, nose in the air. Suddenly, she dashed off, heading back the way they had come. Her white figure vanished around a curve in the road.

"Laitha!" Harry shouted fruitlessly. Ragwort followed a short distance, barking, but quickly gave up and returned to Harry, requesting his afternoon ride.

Harry and Maela exchanged glances. "She shall rejoin us, I am certain," Harry said, ignoring the terrier. They waited for a few minutes, though the horses chafed and fidgeted.

There was crackling of brush, and three armed men leaped from behind trees and into the road. They were filthy, skinny, and ragged, missing many teeth. "Ho, there, guvna'," one shouted, aiming his bow at Harry. "Tarry a season. We would have business with thee."

The other two grinned, eyeing Maela and the horses greedily.

Harry struggled to keep Saul still, repeatedly ordering, "Stand." Calmly, he asked, "What business have we with thee, my good fellow?"

Maela silently prayed, squeezing her eyes shut, peeking between her eyelids.

"Grafton's my name, and daresay I ain't so very good! Dismount, sir. Hawkins, get me the gray," the leader ordered.

One of the men approached King Saul, but Harry warned, "Have a care! He has a wicked kick and would readily bite."

This was news to Maela, but she kept quiet. The horse did look dangerous. His mouth gaped and foamed; he pranced ponderously, ears flattened, eyes rolling. Harry seemed unable to control him.

Hawkins looked to his leader questioningly, but at that moment there was a "thunk" and an arrow appeared in Grafton's breast. Eyes popped wide, he dropped his bow and grasped the arrow with both hands, then crumpled in his tracks.

Hawkins fumbled to load his bow, but stopped when something sharp pressed against the nape of his neck. It was Harry's hunting knife. Dropping the bow and arrow, the would-be thief lifted his hands in submission. "We're lost, Becker."

Laitha sniffed at Becker's worn boots, growling. The thief looked from her to Harry, then beyond Maela, and his hands also lifted.

Maela turned. There, not ten paces away, stood her father with an arrow at the ready, aimed at Becker's heart. "Thy company was greater than we knew," Becker observed. "I like not these odds."

"Coward," Sir Hanover observed without malice. "Shall I shoot the rabble?"

"Nay," Harry replied quietly. "Disarm them and let them go."

"They shall assault another company another day," Trenton reminded him.

"That is not my business. We shall alert the constable at Bourne."

Maela held the horses, allowing them to graze calmly at the roadside while Harry and her father disarmed the thieves and discussed plans. After obsequiously thanking Harry for sparing their lives, Becker and Hawkins disappeared back into the woods, bearing their leader's body between them.

"I must collect my horses," Trenton was saying. "When thy hound came unto me, I ascertained thy need and hastened to aid thee. Unwilling to alert thine assailants, I tethered the horses a short way off and skulked through the trees. I am acquainted with these woods, having hunted here in the past. Thieves abound herein."

Harry thumped Laitha's bony sides, praising her to the skies. "Wise, most excellent dog! You have done us great service this day. Thanks be to God for His timely intervention by means of a lowly dog!"

"And a lowly scoundrel father." Turning to Maela, Trenton lifted his eyes to meet hers. "I desire to make amends to thee, daughter. My heart does rue my past behavior toward thee and toward others of my kindred. During my convalescence, I spoke often and at length with Marston about the duties of a father and of my duty to the Creator. For many years, I did give all to Isaac, believing him my child of promise; yet he did spurn mine attentions. Thou, Ishmaela, child of my true love, I did neglect and disdain. I would ask thy pardon, my dearest, most undeserved child."

A great lump formed in Maela's throat. Pegasus tugged at his rein, trying to reach a tempting weed.

"While I held thee captive at the castle, thy forbearance greatly impressed me; and yet I would not confront mine own heart and see myself as I truly was. I have abused thee, humiliated thee, neglected thee, and intended to ruin thee, yet you have returned unto me only honor and loving-kindness. I have purposed to make restitution unto thee in any manner possible. I observed thy nuptials from hiding and blessed them in my heart; I attempted to guard thee during thy travels, though thy husband has proven himself proficient. He would have outwitted these brigands unassisted in a matter of moments had I not intervened."

Trenton turned to Harry, "A masterful exhibition of horsemanship, I must say, Jameson. Thy steed would have flattened that rogue ere he knew what hit him."

Harry smiled acknowledgment, but remained silent.

Maela's father continued, "I have learned, though late, that God promises fulfillment and love to those who repent and give fealty to Him. With my remaining days upon this earth, I desire to serve Him where'er He leads me. I can only trust that His promises are true."

Hanover's sober expression softened as he gazed at Maela. "Not least among my trials of penance has been the safe conduct of two creatures, which, I have been assured, are dear unto thy heart, my daughter. Why this is so, I cannot imagine, for they have occasioned me labors incalculable these four days."

Trenton looked into his daughter's wondering eyes and smiled. "Tarry here. I shall quickly return." He hurried into the woods.

Harry took Saul's rein and slipped an arm around his wife's waist. "He hungers after thy forgiveness, Maela. Truly, he has endured much for thy sake, as you shall acknowledge upon his return." He hugged Maela close.

She buried her face in his chest, taking comfort from the steady beat of his heart. Harry was easy to love. But did she dare forgive her father and trust him with her love? He was violent, volatile—just now he had killed a man and seemed to think nothing of it! Maela knew she would see Grafton crumple in her nightmares for many nights to come, just as, countless times, she had relived the cold edge of her father's sword at her throat. And yet. . .he had called her dear, apologized humbly, and actually seemed to crave her forgiveness and acceptance.

Hoofbeats upon the road warned them of Hanover's return. Maela faced her father, allowing Harry to take the horses' reins from her. She was acutely aware that these approaching moments represented a turning point in her life.

Trenton dismounted, then carefully lifted a sack from his packhorse. Strange noises emanated from it, almost like. . .

Maela gasped in startled anticipation. She took the proffered bag and loosened its string. Two wobbly heads emerged; enormous golden eyes gazed up at her, then around. "Daisy!" She barely caught the tiger kitten before it sprang to the ground. Giving it a hug and kiss, she shoved it back into the bag and caught up the calico for a moment. "Oh, Lily, my dear!"

Harry helped her confine the frightened kittens once more, then took the bag from her. His smile, overflowing with love and assurance, bolstered her resolve.

Maela approached her father and looked up into his hopeful eyes, seeing her face mirrored in their dark depths. "My father," her voice cracked. She swallowed hard and tried again. "You have my full pardon. I love thee unreservedly, as Jesus Christ loves me."

A moment later she was crushed in strong arms, and a husky voice repeated her name over and over, "Maela! Maela, my little child!"

Harry watched, smiling, swallowing hard. Then Hanover Trenton lifted one arm and drew his new son into the circle, exclaiming, "God is indeed good! As He has promised, so He has done!"

# nineteen

*Praise ye the LORD. O give thanks unto the LORD;*
*for he is good: for his mercy endureth for ever.*
Psalm 106:1

Standing on the quay, Maela wept unreservedly into Harry's jerkin, shivering with sorrow and cold. Chill winter winds cut through her cloak; only when Harry held her close was she warm. The ship had passed out of view, and with it her father. After eight weeks of blessed fellowship, work, and fun spent with Harry's extensive family and his own precious daughter, Hanover Trenton had taken ship for the continent. He could no longer endanger his loved ones' lives by remaining with them.

Harry murmured into his wife's ear, "Let us return to the inn. We can sup and speak more of this in comfort."

Maela managed to tuck away a creditable supper, finding that she did, after all, have an appetite. After finishing his supper, Harry handed meaty bones to the two dogs. Contented growls and crunchings emanated from beneath the table.

"Our home will seem empty without my father," Maela observed, apparently determined to be gloomy. "I am exceedingly grateful that he stayed on past Epiphany and truly fellowshipped with us, but now I shall miss him terribly."

"I am certain we shall not suffer from loneliness. My mother appreciates thy value as willing child-minder, and she certainly enjoys thy company. Now that Rosalind has married and gone to town, Mother needs thy listening ears, my dear."

"I do love thy mother," Maela smiled, but still seemed distracted. "Harry, I must tell thee something of import." Her expression was deadly serious.

He waited, then prompted, smiling, "Which is?"

"I believe Laitha again carries pups by Lord Marston's staghound."

Harry chuckled. "Verily, I know it; but when shall you tell me of our own pup?"

Maela gaped, uncertain whether to laugh or cry. "Wherefore did you discern it?"

Harry smiled lovingly. "You have been violently ill each morn this past fortnight and believed I would suspect nothing?"

She flushed. "Art thou pleased?"

"I could not be more so. My dearest love. . ." He glanced around the crowded room. "Let us hasten to our chambers and discuss this privately." Together, the young couple and their hound left the dining room.

Under the table, Ragwort tugged at his large bone, stopped to stare at it, sighed, then abandoned it to follow his family upstairs.

# A Letter To Our Readers

Dear Reader:

In order that we might better contribute to your reading enjoyment, we would appreciate your taking a few minutes to respond to the following questions. When completed, please return to the following:

Rebecca Germany, Managing Editor
Heartsong Presents
PO Box 719
Uhrichsville, Ohio 44683

1. Did you enjoy reading *A Child of Promise?*
   ❑ Very much. I would like to see more books
      by this author!
   ❑ Moderately
      I would have enjoyed it more if _____

      _____

2. Are you a member of **Heartsong Presents**? ❑Yes ❑No
   If no, where did you purchase this book? _____

      _____

3. What influenced your decision to purchase this
   book? (Check those that apply.)

   ❑ Cover            ❑ Back cover copy

   ❑ Title            ❑ Friends

   ❑ Publicity        ❑ Other_____

4. How would you rate, on a scale from 1 (poor) to 5
   (superior), the cover design? _____

5. On a scale from 1 (poor) to 10 (superior), please rate the following elements.

___Heroine      ___Plot

___Hero      ___Inspirational theme

___Setting      ___Secondary characters

6. What settings would you like to see covered in **Heartsong Presents** books?_____

_____

_____

7. What are some inspirational themes you would like to see treated in future books?_____

_____

_____

8. Would you be interested in reading other **Heartsong Presents** titles?   ❑ Yes      ❑ No

9. Please check your age range:
   ❑ Under 18    ❑ 18-24    ❑ 25-34
   ❑ 35-45    ❑ 46-55    ❑ Over 55

10. How many hours per week do you read? _____

Name _____

Occupation_____

Address_____

City_____ State_____ Zip_____